Street Corner Spirits

poems & flash fiction

Westley Heine

ROADSIDE PRESS

copyright

Dedicated to Andrea Heine who took a lifetime of my poems and edited the first three parts of this collection into a cohesive arc. Friend. Lover. Wife.

Pre-amble

It's always the same old question:
Why write about darkness?
To shed light on darkness.
To enlighten the shadows.
To eliminate ignorance.
To see it and give it a name.
To exorcise darkness and bring it back to the sun.
To balance duality to one.
To make the unknown known.
To see is to understand, relate, forgive, love.
To cleanse with light with a burning passion.
Let it out, define it, and all fear will fade.

Part 1 – Eulogies of Youth

Karaoke

As a kid
I would go to the bars with my Dad, and get bored.
Sure, in Wisconsin you could drink with your parents when you were sixteen,
but drinking beer in that small town just made me feel numb.
Everyone's eyes glossed over while yelling at the Packer Game.
Drinking was more fun when it wasn't allowed, when
I was off under bridges with the boys.

My Dad and I
would play darts or pool.
He would play well and I wouldn't really try.
But we liked to play the jukebox and talk music.
What I really liked was when they had Karaoke.
I never picked the party songs.
You know what I mean: Journey, Bon Jovi, or "Sweet Home Alabama."
I liked to pick the odd songs, the freaky songs, the ones that rang true when I
was off smoking and drinking in graveyards with the boys.

Imagine a group of nice middle-aged Baby Boomers drinking suds, when
a shaggy teenager in black starts singing "When The Music's Over" by The Doors.
My voice was never in tune, just wailing, the annoying adolescent voice cracking.
I was shrieking the drug-soaked songs from their own generation.
Rubbing their faces in their old music was more shocking
than singing something like Marilyn Manson.
They would get anxious and feel all the horror their parents felt.

One time

after singing "White Rabbit" by The Jefferson Airplane, which ends with
the line "Feed your head! Feed your head!" an old fisherman told me, "That
means read more books."

"I read plenty, sir," I responded.

Afterwards, even though I was being a smartass punk,

I would feel very old and very young all at once.

And that

was a good feeling.

Boys and Girls

When I was a boy,
I beat the shit out of another boy,
because he had felt up my girl,
and she was mine.

She told me she was drunk,
so drunk she couldn't move
and he took advantage of her.

Once he was my friend,
now I hated him
with his hair gel, intentional stumble, and trendy clothes.

So during school lunch, as he walked to his nice car,
I jumped on his back
I pushed him down
I spun him around
I hit him in the face again, and again,
until his perfect white teeth went red.

I yelled, "Now stay away from her!"
I left him on the pavement.
My friend Vinny was watching and cheered, "We love you Wes!"
He was oddly excited by the bloodlust.
Hearing the voice, I looked back over my shoulder
my eyes were going in every direction,
half crazy.

Then I went back inside the school.
I sat next to my girlfriend in the cafeteria.
She said, "I knew you cared."

Then I stood up and went to the principle's office, and
turned myself in.

Now, when getting a new job,
I still have to explain this story during background checks.
I tell the story just like that: as if I was some kind of
vigilante defending a young woman's honor.
But the truth is,
later on she told me she wasn't drunk.
She had kissed him back.
The boy I beat and I were friends again before I even went to court.
The girl would be with someone else by the time I was in jail.
And before she cheated on me with the guy I hit,
I had cheated on her…
Secretly I just wanted to see what it was like to set all my anger free.
I wasn't just mad at the other boy.
I wasn't just mad at her.
I was mad at myself.
I was mad.
I was a boy.
I was not yet
a man.

Peach Schnapps

The first time I got drunk was when
I found a plastic bottle of Peach Schnapps sitting in the parking lot
of a bowling alley in Wisconsin.
I was 13 and had a Metallica T-shirt for every day of the week.
I pocketed it and called my friend Marcy on a payphone.
It was 1997. She walked over.
We went to the graveyard the only place the living could be alone in town.
We sipped the sweet flowery syrup.
It tasted like peach bubble gum rather than real peaches.
The sun was bright and hot.
The rays went straight through my skull
as if God were touching my brain.
I laughed and danced.
Marcy rolled her eyes but smiled.
As we walked down the sidewalk I rubbed against the hedges,
and felt the leaves scratch against me.
It was bliss to be young, high, and free.
Everything was possible.
It seemed all the young dreams were going to come true.
I was wrong.
I grew up to be a corporate drone like everyone else.
And Marcy killed herself a few years ago.
I've been getting drunk ever since that day in 1997, and
I hate the taste of Peach Schnapps.

My Soul

There was always a sense of competition
between JT and me.
When I first came to town, JT felt that his spot in the gang of outsiders was
threatened.
Out of the clump of scraggly metal-head kids in middle school
JT and I were the only ones who tried in class.
The others saw academics as part of the world, which was to be rejected.
JT and I tried to do well, determined to be book smart as well as street smart.
In fact, books were the only way to escape the little town.

It was the late 1990s and *The Simpsons* was the only show on TV that told the truth.
There was a classic episode where Bart disputes the existence of his soul and sells it
to Millhouse by writing on a plain piece of paper: This is Bart Simpson's Soul.
After the episode aired I told the guys that I would do it.
If anyone had some cash I would fork over my soul.
We were sitting in the cafeteria and everyone checked their pockets.
JT was the highest bidder: he had a five-dollar bill.
So I drafted up the contract: Westley Heine's Soul goes to JT for $5.
JT seized the piece of paper and folded it neatly in the pocket of his jeans.

Soon JT was different.
By high school he stopped wearing heavy metal T-shirts.
He began listening to rap instead.
He tried his hand at drug dealing and got a pager.
He still tried at school but his grades began to slip.
By the time he moved from dealing weed to coke JT was totally transformed.
He began wearing all white: a white track suit, white shoes, and
a white baseball cap cocked to one side.
He wanted to be called JT Money.
He would pull out his bills and count 'em at you.

We would call him JT Phony behind his back.

He got this pleasant preppy girl Rebecca on the white stuff.

She got more ditzy and looked more and more like a skeleton.

Last I heard he moved on to heroin, got busted, and did a stint in the State Pen.

Now, I'm not a superstitious person.

Otherwise I would have never sold my soul for five bucks in the first place.

But at dark times, in the throws of my own struggles with alcohol and adult life,

it has crossed my mind to ask JT for my soul back.

I mean it couldn't hurt…

But considering how much worse he has had it since we were kids

I think I will be better off if JT just kept my stinking soul.

I've long since spent the five bucks.

Duster

I've had the shakes.
I've puked red.
I've stayed up all night waiting for the acid to wear off.
I've huffed gas, and saw spots turn to little green men.
I've smoked joints soaked in pen ink for some reasonless reason.
One night I did too much coke and sat in a cold shower holding my chest.

But there was only one time that I really felt scared, when I thought I
might actually die.
I went through the curtain into the attic bedroom.
The walls were hand painted and the floor green shag.
A girl with a shaved head, Angel, had a can of Duster wrapped in a towel.
Duster is the shit office people spray to clean keyboards.
She inhaled and her usual soft voice came out as low Barry White.
She spoke with no words just, "Whomp, whomp, whaaaa," like a sad trombone.
Then she laughed like it was the first laugh of a child.

She passed the can of Duster to Nigel who
explained, "It changes the density of your vocals chords."
He took a hit and passed it to Caleb.
I, an artist, took out my small digital camera and started filming.
Anthony came into the room and swiped my camera away as I took the
can of Duster.
I placed the towel over it.
I found one of the last dry spots that no one's lips had touched (you have
to be health conscious of you know…) flipped the nozzle, and heaved in
the chemical.
I inhaled a long time. I didn't know how long to hit.
Nigel prodded, "Oh man, Wes is gonna fuckin trip!"
Anthony turned the camera on me.
He started filming me and rhymed, "West always thinks he's the best.
Watch him go!"

With my one free hand I flipped him off and then tried to grab the
camera back.
He resisted and I let up from the duster can.
Just then Caleb stumbled by and fell flat on the coffee table spilling cans
and ashtrays.

A sharp cold sting rose through the center of my brain.
Someone was feeling vintage because Alice Cooper was on the record
player.
It didn't matter what was playing because soon the music was unrecognizable.
All the sounds in the room began to feedback inside my brain.
The tones took on a monotonous insect drone that pulsed without form.
My right and left-brain seemed to cross wires, scattering all the input.
I finally did it, I thought.
I finally broke something. This doesn't feel like it will go away.

According to the footage I stood up and said, "I feel like I'm going to die."
I grasped at the camera again but Anthony held tight.
I flopped back in a chair and said, "Well, if I'm going to die you might as
well film it."
I slid my fingers over my face and then looked up and smiled.
Then effects began to wear off.
Nigel looked up from picking up Caleb's mess and asked, "You alright Wes?"
"Yeah, I'll be alright."
"Oh good." Then in a game show announcer voice Nigel said, "You
handle your inhalants well!"
"I don't handle anything well," I said.
Anthony looked for the off switch on the camera. "How do I stop this?"
he asked.
I asked, "How do you stop what?"
"How do you stop THIS?"
Our vocal chords froze.
The question fed back.
The sound echoed in my skull.

Meaning crossed wires.
Then everyone laughed.
I laughed too.

Rain Dance

"Hear that?" She turned toward the window.
"That's thunder!" She pulled back the curtain.
"The sky is cracking!" She looked at me.
I must have been acting gloomy because I couldn't play outside.

"Come on! Let's go see!" I started to tie my shoes.
"You don't need those! Let's go!"
She took my hand and pushed past the screen door.
Just in time rain began to fall from the grey sky.

Barefoot we ran across the lawn. We ran into the hayfield.
The rain was warm. Lightning shot gold in the distance.
She spread her arms and spun around. I did the same.
Her wide smile was drenched. Her long black hair was dripping.

She laughed for joy. I jumped up and down and laughed too.
She taught me summer rain was our friend, and that
how we felt had more to do with what was inside us,
rather than what was happening in the world on the outside.

She was up, she was down, but this is when I loved her best:
arms outstretched with the electricity branching behind her.
This is when I wasn't afraid of anything.
I was six years old, and she was my mother.

Scarecrow Joe

Joe ---- could be seen around town on his paper route or collecting cans. His tongue would be sticking out sideways, and his eyes swimming around. In a town full of dopey characters, Joe was something else. He was in his early twenties, but he played with sticks and rolled down grassy hills.

Once my little metal-head friends and I were mucking around on our bikes looking for a place to smoke weed when Joe ----- chased us down. He turned slightly, put his hand to his mouth, and made a static noise like he was on a walkie-talkie. Then he said, "Those are my men. They're coming for you guys!"

"Shut-up, Joe!"

"Yeah, get the fuck out of here Joe!"

One day I was driving with my dad and we passed Joe as he was talking to a Christmas tree that was left on the curb. "There's Joe -----" I said.

"Joe -----?" asked my dad. "That boy's still alive?"

"Yeah, he's something like the village idiot."

But my dad didn't laugh. And my dad loves to laugh. Instead he got serious. "I worked with his father, Brett ----, at the steel yard. This was before you were born. I was at the bar when Brett came in. He just had a baby so we were surprised to see him out. He was crying and shaking. He couldn't put two words together. Finally, after a few stiff shots of rye Brett explained. He had hired a babysitter for his baby

Joe while he was working the night shift. Apparently Joe wouldn't stop crying. So the babysitter put the little baby in the microwave and turned it on."

I told my friends not to swear at Joe anymore, even if he was annoying.

Bomb

The loudspeaker at the high school announced: Everyone is to evacuate.

I was glad to leave. It was my senior year and I was fighting with my girlfriend again.

"A bomb? Who cares?" I thought. Somehow, my young brain thought I was ready to die, but really I was ready to be reborn and get out of that little town. Leaving the building was good enough for now.

The police arrived with a bomb-sniffing dog. Outside on the curb I ran into the chemistry teacher Mr. Burbank. He was eccentric. He brewed his own moonshine in the chemistry lab. Once he chased away some pro-life extremists handing out pamphlets full of pictures of dead fetuses while the kids were waiting for the bus. There on the curb he told me, "Even if the cops clear us to go inside we're going to have class outside today. I'm not taking any chances."

The loud speaker went off again. Everyone was called inside to the auditorium. I waved to Mr. Burbank who stayed on the curb with his arms crossed. On the way inside my girlfriend caught up with me. She was trying to talk to me about something. It was something important, important to her at least. I didn't care anymore. I ran away from her. She thought she could treat me like I was like one of her younger brothers. She reached towards me and ripped my T-shirt. We looked crazy acting that way during the bomb drama, but love is more important than death.

The principle addressed the student body. It unraveled that someone had written "Bomb in Building" on a toilet stall in the boy's bathroom. I felt that I looked like the guilty party with my freshly torn shirt. I found out later that my friend Derek was the one who found the microscopic inscription in the bathroom. He told me, "I was taking a deuce and then I saw that. I thought this is one way to get out of my fucking math test."

As the principle spoke he kept saying, "It's one of you. It's one of you." That year I was on the yearbook committee. It seemed like an easy credit. As the principle spoke I remembered that some poor schmuck had to airbrush a photo of the principle's son because his kid had decided to flash his shaft out during a group picture. Any other kid would have been expelled. Meanwhile, we all had to sit there solemnly because someone made a dumb joke about a bomb on a bathroom wall. I began to feel bad. I felt bad for all the real school shootings. I felt bad for all the lessons we were missing. I felt bad about the lesson the principle was trying to teach us now though it wasn't the one he thought he was teaching us.

The principle kept saying, "It's one of you. It's one of you." Part of me wished there was a bomb, a real threat, so we didn't have to feel so stupid. To hell with him and his dumb fear. To hell with his son's dumb shaft. To hell with the empty promise that our lives mattered. Oh the children! Of course our lives mattered, just not yet. I couldn't wait to leave town.

Eulogies of Youth

   Us kids

hiding, hanging out, going home.
  Behind abandoned buildings, in graveyards,
   inside basements below dreaming parents with heads
full of stone,
  vodka stolen from liquor cabinets now watered down and
useless, kissing games, séances, smoldering sex experiments
    leaning back into a buzz of cola, glue, and
  perfume.

     Hiding
    hanging out, holding hands, going
  home,
  holding bags of weed in crotches and bras.
Gangs on foot in a daze crosstown.
  Solders fighting themselves,
   casualties of boredom, slit eyed in the sun
  behind the veil of main street,
    in empty factories,
   under bridges down by the reeds,
  wandering along railroad tracks between drainage
  ditches, and
 composts of death.
   In haylofts, in cars propped up on cinder-blocks,
    smoking in superstitious circles, drinking in
    animal rows,
   tripping in alien fields.

Us kids
that threw rocks off the over-pass for laughs and regrets.
We who told crumpled old couples:
"Turn on your radio, didn't you hear? It's World
War Three!"
We who got drunk at parties screaming:
"I've been touched by God, now I'm pressing charges."
Sailors on seas of acid trails,
partying through the redeyes of
consequence.
(Do you remember when we preached that there was no God?)

In towns too small for our hearts,
orange autumn evenings smoldering in the haze of
streetlights,
crushed butterflies, dead leaves, and lungs sipping cool air.
At thirteen I came into myself, or something came into me.
All the perfect crimes I was nostalgic for, even
as I did them.
The insane urge to fix the world by destroying it.
The typical non-conventional symptom: rebellion against the idea of
"normal,"
which never really existed.
In suburbs where they cut down trees and name streets after them:
Elm St, Maple St, Pine Grove

Us kids
crowded in cornfields sharing bottles of paint.
Parts of cars spread out in yards like space-age
sculptures,
spliced together as fire breathing demons,
off to cruise for chicks and roadkill.
(Only the eye in the sky knows what happens during our blackouts.)

Us Punks
who slunk around smashing in windows, and pissing squirt gun fights.
Crack and glue parties at the playground,
slums of car door slams, and
hinges creaking out the scarecrow violin blues.

Us kids

out the window

escaping by bike pedal, the swamp fog lit gold by the
harvest moon, the smell of yeast and mint all around in great
singing freedom.
Up drainage pipes into Romeo like windows surrounded by
ceremonial candles.
Making love in golf courses,
graveyards, cars, swimming holes, and
locker rooms
and off to the prom on ecstasy even hugging the principal.

We that bit the hand that fed us, and spit in the face of morning.
We that made fun of everything, even ourselves.
That split hairs about music genre until the sound was
reduced to infinity.
That were set up and busted down.
That headbutted windshields and picked metallic
psychological scabs.
That made bonfires in the swamp,
blew off M-80s,
raided the campgrounds like Vikings
in search of free beer and wild girls.

Us kids

who crashed daddy's truck over the Christmas tree,
exploded cattails with revolvers,
shot up between toes, snorted coke off tractor tails,
and passed out in the fridge on Oxycotin.
That slammed booze, got beaten till sober,
then threw skateboards out the car window laughing sick.
That spit pennies while pulled over.
That went straight edge and back again.
That starved themselves with Vegan morality.
That spoke of peace with the Anarchist Cookbook under arm,
and finally passed out while slinging the soul
out over the stoic garage band crowd
too cool for life.

Us that moshed in the school hallway.
That smoked cigarettes soaked in ink and laced
with ground up hemp necklaces in a vain attempt to see.
Whose sarcasm beat the dead horse, re-opened wounds, and shredded the machine.
Saying bottoms up, and bottomed out, blacked out,
and back again not afraid to face the fire.
That in one day got an abortion, made the gig, got in a fight, and hosted a party holding back hair as innocence was puked out raw.
We that shot our mouths off, and got a shot in the mouth.
That ate shrooms in the haunted forest, and acid on the Indian burial ground.
Our innocent faces that started to look like another grunge rocker's hairball,
and believed that they were reincarnations of blood spitting idols.
That hocked at the ceiling, eyes sealed from vodka, challenging God to step outside and finally finish it all.

We that danced in traffic at dawn.

That told cops that their lights were trippy.

Whose hometowns got bypassed by the future.

See the neon up there on the vast superhighway?

As the factories closed,

as the prices went up,

we always wanted the system to fall, but

who knew that it would take itself down,

and that we would care?

Cheers to my friend that dressed in a military surplus uniform an

went down to the bar to get free drinks as Iraq was invaded,

and to the cross eyed mumbling men toasting the

surface reality and slapping down cash for the brave boy in drag

My friends who were so crazy they didn't even know they were poets.

Who lost their masks at midnight UNable to shave off the spirits,

then singing and crying on the floor when they finally did find themselves.

Us drugged up and wide eyed children witnessing the wondrous

mystery.

Us bouncing between naughty brats scheming a prank,

and hollow Buddhas weeping and laughing in the pit.

Vibrating with porch bands, basement bands, bowling alley bands,

that found the devil first (low register Ohm exorcism)

and only knew then

that God must be real as well,

and all at once.

Us kids
who wrote poems in jail as if in a monastery for the damned.
That moved to slums despite middleclass comforts and Norman Rockwell roots.
That drank till we were numb then beat each other like flirting brothers.
That scattered senses with 100 watt bulbs and speed metal in little white rooms.
That spoke in backward sentences with true logic of the human heart.
That trashed the homes of hosts who over apologized for the way things looked.
That slid down stairs to vomit peanut brittle on silver platters desperate for more time.

Who had hallucinogenic parties in dorms.
Drove the Buick to St. Louis, spitting fire out the
tailpipe, where it finally blew up taking the train to Chicago chased by tornados
like thought bubbles.
That gambled their lives jumping off stages, rafters, skateboards,
the backs
of bleachers, and railroad bridges.
That mocked their own generation's attempt to matter in history, and
dissolved into a pool of eternity on the carpet.

Moaning
the next verse to the same old song,
the next movement in an ancient unconscious pulse like
the weeping sound of stars falling, the sliding streetlight trombones
the wailing feedback of whiny existential alley cats,
of cowboy goat men, and leather clad bats
all blowing smoke ring echoes, howling out a hollow halo.
First unaware of our harmonies with the past,
of chorus's repeating, of antecedents, boomers, beats, bohemians,
all lost generations
tired, tried, played out, on repeat waiting for the next life,
restlessly dying too soon
only to reincarnate forever.

Us punks
spoiled… pickled… impaled on the sky
weaned on gutter consumerism
nursed on gas station culture
laughing at mirrors and fisting windows.
That drank to sleep,
that would rather dream with the dead than live in society,
that huffed gas faster than a SUV,
that made points about god with double negative speech negating
linear time.
Senseless
sensory overload
who while cackling madly chased friends with a bloody syringe.
That set off fireworks in intersections, blew up
mailboxes, and
paint balled pedestrians.
That ran away to live in empty factories, graveyards, on
couches,
counting coins at midnight by candlelight.
That safety pinned their foreskin,
sold plasma for a bus ticket,
puked philosophy up from the floor,
onto the couch
over the TV fuzz
and out the door.

Who paid for prostitutes all night just to hear
their sad stories.
Who woke bums and asked them to go skateboarding.
An invisible tribe too ironic to even fit in with the
counterculture.

Us kids, growing old, going home
that chewed dildos and spit the pieces across the room onto quieter
conversations.
That broke into the dentist office and stole the laughing gas for raving reflections.
That danced in traffic over lost love, headlights blurred by tears and screams.
That pushed the rabbit-hole of cynicism to
its end exploding in deasix-macina.
That sought god, which was
just under the nose, warm around the
peripheral, and under the tongue

Us kids
hiding, hanging out, going home.
Who were so full of life because they hadn't yet lived.
That grew up too fast by acting young.
That feasted at the root of the Earth, now wide eyed on the other side.
Who are still laughing, still smiling
emanating frozen love forever
without fear.

Part 2 – Between the Cracks

A Hermit in the City

      I can still see him
down there
scurrying along the floor
like dried fruit,
      clutching his bottle,
      peeking over the windowsill
at orgasms and train-wrecks,
down
in his cozy little rut.

      I look at him
through the vent in his ceiling,
my floor.
      He doesn't know that I watch,
      but I can tell
he senses me.

      We live on great steps
      under the ocean,
      on tectonics of grease
        sliding over
        suns of lava,
      a coral reef of glass buildings,
      plastic gardens,
      and cement beams of energy.

      As I stare
he becomes more excited, more nervous.
      He scuttles across the floor

trying to find out
where he is.
        Even though,
he's always been in the same place,
        and so have I.

Blue Island

Spools of razor wire tumbleweeds fall off freights like broken dreams.
Spokes ping-pong in songs of children now too old for tinker bells.

Oil pools pocket the raped surface of the factory-infested moon.
Overpasses and Indian trails crisscross in electric salad.

Why do I have nostalgia for somewhere I never was?
It chews the spirit clear.

The TV sings recession, but I sit and sigh watching history repeat.
Below is the valley full of echoes of the dead.

A Room Full of Paper Souls

Little black dress: out-to-be-in.
She has some tonic with a pinch of gin.

I strike up a match, in with the fold.
Got a paper cut from my money roll.

Small talk with paper dolls.
I would love you but you have no flaws.

Dog-eared days, same old page.
Read it so much it's thin as cellophane.

One problem at a time, or one after another?
One day at a time as the nights blur together.

The bottle never makes it to the shelf.
The glass is half empty cause we're full of ourselves.

Heaven has a headache. It starts to split.
When I'm at the gates please acquit.

Cracks in the pavement, we live between.
This shallow world is only skin deep.

You know that you loved me, but you never felt at home.
Now that you're gone you live in my bones.

Less is more, more or less.
It is what it is, though it could be better.

Revolution, round and round.
Molotov Cocktail gets you high, burns you down

A well of angels stirs in my drink.
Life flashes between every blink.

Plasma Deluge

What do you do when everything's been done?
Who are you when you see that we're all one?

Where do you go God when you are everywhere?
It must be lonely being everywhere...

All the fleeting forms decay as they feed,
a slow motion dance their tentacles weave.

Prosthetic spirits poured into flesh.
Strap-on souls stagger forward.

Sheets of rain illuminate the forlorn holographic people
as moonlight strikes them parallel to their jagged angles.

And cheerful demons sit and kick their calves out over the vine
covered bridges on the riverfront where the medieval city drains its
sewage like a freshly lacerated vein.

Am I even here?
Or infinity in a mirror?

Digital World

In a digital world—
There are pictures but no photography.
In a digital world—
Everyone is on the phone but no-one talks.
In a digital world—
We forget our bloodstream is analogue.
In a digital world—
We think everything is better, but we're just quicker at being bad.
In a digital world—
Everything could be automated, workers set free, but
we're just expected to do more in less time.
In a digital world—
Music is just background noise.
In a digital world—
No one knows the names of their favorite songs.
In a digital world—
Nine year olds are watching porn.

Rave 2003

A dimly lit warehouse filled with gutter-punks and E-tards,
all squirming in a greasy ameba group.
A moaning cocoon of Vaseline and piercings
blurting out lisps of love and laughter.
Pools of unwashed clothes and good intentions.
A pincushion pussy burping out contagious catchphrases,
scarecrows and gargoyles,
plastic fantastic voodoo girls,
a meaningless mess clinging for substance,
crying in my ambiguous soul.

Perfect Moment

Maybe 2004 or 2005?
We woke up early
entwined on my single mattress
tucked in my studio apartment
wrapped in my hairy white legs
coiled in your smooth brown haunches
your eyes shaped like tear drops
blinked awake…
Then we rolled up the window and breathed in the clean air
from Lake Michigan blowing through Uptown Chicago.
For breakfast we sipped the pink wine left in the jug after the night
before
as "Red Shoes" by Tom Waits oozed from my stereo.
You cocked your glorious behind in the air
elbows on the blue mattress
eyes looking off to the side
a smile to nowhere.
As your pendulum swayed to the music
your wondrous hips eclipsed the moon.
I placed my hand on your orbs just to feel you slide across my palm
as you pivoted so graceful, alive, uncaring.
Then you grabbed your big black leather purse, and went off
to the boutique in Boystown to help drag-queens transform.
We didn't make love that morning because
we had exhausted ourselves the night before.
Yet this was somehow better.
I loved you. You knew it.
So I never told you
until it was too late…

But this was a perfect moment—
hypnotizing…
There are so few perfect moments.
So simple.
So rare.
I just had to tell you.

Street Corner Spirits

The city sounds like an ocean
as cars cut the inky night and streetlamps dance underwater.
Orange windows full of sleeping skulls sway in the haloed Chicago sky.
Ten years ago we were just kids pretending to be grown up.
We spent neon evenings burning chemicals through the forehead.
I could barely stand myself slumped in the corner naked giggling
holding back insecurity.
We hid together, broke, dreaming of wild years to come.
We cruised the freeway looking for what would be our has-been
nights.
We crouched in murky rooms drinking away the humidity and
toasting rain.
We fell in love, but we didn't tell each other because we were too cool.
We screamed and yawned at those who dared to play it safe,
who dared to waste their lives by building them.
I spent forever contemplating eternity, and each moment trying to
blackout.
I've wasted my life trying to find the meaning of life.

Now, I drown in layers of irony and contradiction.
I've wiped my ass with angels and spent years trying to forgive myself.
I sat in alleys beating a drum while monkeys chewed money grinning.
You sucked the fire out of my belly and I gave you the salt of the
Earth.
Your diamond chin slept in my thighs and we had the same dream
that night.
I cried all over you like a baby breastfeeding.
You still think there's a future,
and no matter how much I drink I still have all the memories.

Even now, a bottle is being rubbed like a genie lamp as I awake after
midnight.
Nothing has changed, but everything is different.
Another lost night finding only myself.
We always knew it would end ugly like this, but
we're still surprised.

This city incubates our madness.
These streets have the ghosts of our former selves on each corner
waiting for
a bus, hailing a cab, kissing goodbye not knowing it's our last time.
(Eating a meal with something on your mind.)
We've become our real selves,
and no longer care about the novelty of what our real selves might
look like.
We're not gonna die before we're thirty anymore.
We're there.
Gotta think of something more to do.
We've survived.
We're free and
not afraid of anything.

Passing a Girl in Mexico City

She still has her dolls in her closet.
She still looks left then right when crossing a one-way.
She has a dog with no manners.
She'd rather smile than bother.

She has soaps unpronounceable.
She has subtitles in her dreams.
She lets her hair down when her mother isn't around.
She pisses politely.

She thinks Christ is sexy, but
the Father turns her stomach.
She is waiting to be herself,
now that innocence is falling away.

Freak Kingdom

They all end up here
schizos, shape-shifters,
like bugs to light they flock to Hollywood.
They come here, or go to Area 51
following the clues on the screen.

Failed actors, failed street performers, failed street people,
chameleons with no shade, the sun has shined through.
Dreamers outshining the stars as
palm-trees explode like fireworks.

There's a homeless man on the curb wearing a VR headset.
He's somewhere else sitting in a pile of loose ends.

The bleach blonde frozen on the corner like a statue is
wearing a Santa hat and a ballet dress.

The skinny black man sounding the alarm in the street is
wearing a sombrero and a sash, fingers dangling like candles.

At night the houses in the Hollywood Hills flicker.
The porch lights mingle up to the stars.
Meanwhile we drag our knuckles down in the valley below and
stare up at the homes of the rich with the same
bewilderment as peering into the center of the galaxy.
Staring into a world equally mysterious and unattainable
heads full of dreams.
I wonder
if I'm too insane to be an artist, or
not insane enough.

They all come here.
They all end up here,
and so have I.

Just a Bar

These days,
it's hard to find a bar that's just a bar.
Now all the bars have a theme: sports bars, foodie bars, live music,
DJs,
and they serve sugary drinks, or craft beers that taste like wood.

In East Hollywood there are still a few places
where the only sign is a neon that says: Cocktails.
The windows are bricked up and the walls are painted black.
Where we can sit in the darkness.
Where we can sit in the silence.
Where we can sit alone, together.
Where we can sit and drink,
no excuses,
no shame,
in peace.
It's just a bar.

Freeway?

So much space,
full of metal.
So many people,
racing themselves.
Spots open and close.
Cars jut in and out,
a sea of violence.
Cutting in,
cutting out,
almost sexual.
A space opens,
a space fills,
then two idiots ruin it
for the rest of us.
Metal against metal,
bone against bone.
Now we're stopped,
waiting for the tow,
waiting for the cops,
waiting to go home
to eat, sleep, and then
do it all over again.
Insurance and lawyers
betting against blood.
Gambling against sorrow,
betting against salvation,
that comes with new
technology or transportation.
A new way to get there, or
a new way to just stay home.

Green Dawn

Dawn burns away the morning mist.
Car fumes raise green mirages,
striped teeth, oily rainbows, lens flares split like
butterfly wings in the peripheral.
I drive on streets in a grid of neon plaid
channeled through ancient ideas.
My eyes are steaming tears and dewy dreams.
Palm trees punctuate paradise
as the homeless of Hollywood,
grocery carts full of empty bottles of champagne,
recycle the glass of last night's toasts.
The world starts over again,
with or without you.

Like The Grapes of Wrath

I've seen them
picking vegetables in the fields,
like the Grapes of Wrath, and
picking metal in alleys.
Brown faces,
white shirts,
working lawns,
working ten times harder for a fraction of the pay.

I've seen them
celebrating the 4th of July,
X-mas,
Thanksgiving,
louder and bigger than the rest
like they mean it.

I've seen them
sing together,
work together.
They can fix a car themselves, stick to a budget, eat for less, and
all the things us spoiled children had to learn too late.

Cleaning Out a Storage Unit

The sun is warm,
though so far away.
I love the day,
because of the night.
A miracle.

Harvest Day

Every Wednesday is
harvest day on our block.
After fighting through traffic
the parking by my building gets scarce
on Wednesday
because the garbage cans
are out in front of the curb
taking up the spots.

Once the sun goes down,
I can hear it: the squeak of a grocery-cart,
my recycling bin being opened,
and my bottles collected for scrap by the homeless.
Clink, clink, *smash!*
Sometimes the cans and glass wake me.
I get up and look out the window.
I see the streetlights glow on the huddled flesh,
a person living in the shadows we usually ignore.
The police lights down the block strobe that
sick glow on my walls.
It's harvest time.
I think of all my bottles of beer from the week that
have helped me get over my hard work, and helped me
live with myself as I pay for this room.
Toasts of joy, and hits of sorrow,
to feel something, or feel nothing at all.
Yet this is the best feeling: knowing that I am giving something back,
even if it's just bottles to be recycled for a few bucks per pound.
Now someone on the street can get a meal, or
just as likely get more bottles.

Now, I've been a bum.

I've played guitar on the corner for change.

I've slept in warehouses, and on a scaffolding in the rain.

But that was a long time ago.

Now I work in an office where no one has any idea who I was.

Sure, I live in a cheap room just above the curb, but

I play the game to stay in it… and I no longer need to bother

to turn in my own bottles for change anymore.

I can let them go

to the homeless army who rule the streets of LA.

Every Wednesday is

harvest day on our block.

Sugar Skull

Dark avenues
like red tunnels
telescope back
into her inner eye.
Streetlights bend in
the steam of
frying bat meat.
Motel shadows
full of eyes suspend
hidden deals in
cultural force-fields.
Bugs pour from the
cracks in the mirror that
line her face with age.

She was sure she could
lead the homeless army
over the wall of the
Hollywood Forever Cemetery
to dig up the Pharaoh
and use his skull
like a radio to free
the internet slaves.
It was snowing
dope in the desert
all fangs numb
with angel feathers.
She sneezed and
blew her cover
so the cameras

descended on her
and x-rayed her soul
until she believed
she never had one.
She thought if she could
reincarnate into her enemy
and then commit suicide
she could loop time back
to before the world
was poisoned like a well.
Smoking looms of
memories flashed like
lightning in the fog
and burned her silhouette across
the back wall of the Circle-K.
After her paranoid poems were rejected
for channeling the dead she intoned them
like stand-up comedy to her doctors
who decided to laugh rather
than stroke their beards, and
declared her cured, and
shaved their goats, and
bottled her tears, and
sold self-help books based on
the social media version of herself
with a close up of her
carbon footprint on the book jacket.

Pungent flowers will grow from the decay of
her good intentions, blocked orgasms,
confabulated glory days, menstrual sunsets,
lying pen-pals, parent expectations,

self-inflicted lobotomies, fever halos,
conspiracies with the moon, apocalyptic codes,
bonfires with the damned, the eulogy she wrote herself,
her caramelized brain, garbage islands,
melting mushrooms, elephants in the room,
dental dams, teddy bears, street corner prophets,
endless lists of regurgitated objectivity,
and personal madness giggling like
musical rubber numbers under the shade of time.

Will we ever sleep again?
Will we ever dream in a new language?
Will we ever be able to change the world but
preserve our precious melancholy mythology?
Or can peace only arrive through desolation?
Can we through trial and error,
checks and balances, be crowned with utopia
teetering on the peak of
this round of recorded history?
Torn by time, skinless, stretched
on the rack of the sun wheeling in slow motion,
teeth shattered in TV static. Shhhh, it (or god) says.

Part 3 – Peace Within the Void

The Wall

They always said this would happen: the body just hits a wall.
All the old farts and successful men,
all those that survived their younger selves,
they bored me about how this day would come.
But I never thought I would live this long.
Those days when I had energy to burn:
I was on fire with anger and Eros.
Partying seven days in a row, staying up all night and still talking
brilliant shit until 3 pm the next day, or at least everything sounded
brilliant by that point.
The world slowed and glowed.
The trees waved back.
Pine bows turned into pagodas.
The stars would scream.

Now the whisky doesn't hit right, pot makes me paranoid,
uppers make me nervous, and downers will put me in a coma.
Stomach acid crawls up my throat like some toothy
multi-eyed dragon grasping at planets
coming back for revenge for pouring booze on my inner child.

Once, I was a mythological creature.
From Wisconsin to Mexico I was unquenchable.
As I drank molten mirrors
I was indestructible.
Then I hit the wall.
It was sometime in Chicago in that one-room apartment,
drinking straight whisky all day, hair grown out from laziness,
finger tips purple, becoming one with the sunlight…

The booze wasn't fuel for fire anymore, but mud in my capillaries,
beer bubbles would pop into tears,
every morning shaking and spitting green bile.

I hit the wall.
It wasn't just the body that was worn out.
All the dreams flattened: music business, art shows, little independent
movies I made,
there was nothing left to be disillusioned about.
I thought I had done all the right things: I pushed my senses to see
visions. I plunged into drama, laughter, sorrow, life and death.
I organized it all and re-wrote it until it made sense.
All a reflection of eternity, the same old truth, a glimmer of
an apocalypse that no one wants to hear.

My heart crashed against bricks, too.
Not worth the effort and games…
All the girls were crazy, or just not crazy about me.
Or they liked parts of me, slices of me, wanted to cut off pieces of me
a-la cart,
prune, splice, and make me into who they thought they could love.
Just another wall I stopped beating my chest against, no more games,
and no more kinky hang-ups or failed experiments anymore.
I numbed my manhood with whisky until I had no desire.
I stopped trying.

I was tired, dry, flat, pale.
I hit the wall.
But I'm lucky.
I survived.
No more girls, I have a woman now.
No more dreams, I have reality now.
No more whisky binges, just good beer with quality over quantity.

No more madness, death, fanged clowns, just sunrises and
sunsets, three meals a day, and some forgiveness.
My words are heard now, no longer slurred in surrealism.
I sleep better.
I'm on the other side of the wall now.
All that is left,
all that is here,
on this side
of the wall
is love.

Love

hot cement
after rain
cool night breeze
streets are
neon mirrors
gutters filled with rainbow
the smell of
ozone
clean dirt
burning mist
my love & I walking
looking for ice cream
streetlights spin as the
rotating door reflects the
history of the world in the haze
ghosts flash between blinks
laughing because we're in love
the poor slouching Earth is
green with rust
the air is wet with heat
my heart is at rest
finally

Broke

My wife and I went out for dinner.
I got up and went to the bathroom.
Sitting there
my brain reminded me
to steal the roll of toilet paper for home,
but then I remembered
I didn't need to do that anymore.

    If you've ever really been broke it changes you.
    I know how to eat on five bucks a day.
    I know how to make a mop out of old socks.
    I find myself being thrifty like a depression-era grandpa.

Now
I feel guilty paying a fat bill at a nice restaurant.
How was I talked into coming here?
I'm no foodie.
I just want to get full, and
it doesn't matter from what,
or where.

    I graduated from college just as the 2008 recession hit.
    I played guitar on the corner for change.
    I still pick up pennies on the sidewalk.
    And they say my generation is entitled.

Cubicle Matthew

Outside,
the sun is shining,
but we sit in a large whitewashed room
with no windows,
crunching on computers, heads wired to phones clamoring
in cubicles like caged rabbits,
waiting to see who will
snap.

Everyone thought Matthew would go first.
He rushed around nervous and intense.
He wore the same thing everyday: faded black slacks and
a grey shirt buttoned up tight to his Adams-apple.
He was tall and skinny with a head too big for his body.
And he had pop-eyes, and
a five-o-clock shadow which gave his pale face
a slight hint of
green.

And he ate raw pumpkin for lunch everyday.
On Mondays he'd carry a stack of Tupperware from his bellybutton to
his chin
full of pumpkin,
and by Friday it smelled bad when
he popped open the lid.

Now Matthew seemed very intelligent, but was awkward with people.
He stuttered during small talk.
And his hair was always wet
either wet from being washed, or wet from being dirty.

Needless to say no one invited him for drinks at the TJI Fridays across
the office park.

Yet, when the executives from corporate came in to say that there
would be layoffs,
it was Matthew who stood up and said, "You're all fucking bullshit!"
Then
everyone could relate.

Underwater Moon

    Inky waves
weave moonlight in
silver word-smoke,
kinetic calligraphy,
ribbon dances and
jokes with no meaning.
    Electric lassos
choke time into
a tapestry of cherubs
in test tubes,
tide pools and
tear ducts.
    Whips of light
encode whispers of
eternity in sparks,
pictographs of dust, a
zoetrope of train windows
flicker by like burning film.
    Blue halos burst
out the spinal column like
an echo taking light-years
reflecting back to the
source of creation to
confirm all is alive.
    Heartbeat like
sonar to define the void,
a moot-point rectified to
ecstatic revelation like a
a chant echoing down the
halls of history.

Underwater moon
wanes like a pendulum,
a pupil rolling across the
jelly meniscus above
the silent desert made of
the snow of eroded cities.
	I write my name
in the sand and realize it
does not mean a thing
long before it blows away.
And that is the
greatest gift of all.

My Dog

Sometimes, when my wife is out of town,

I sit at home

and look at the other side of the couch,

at her dog,

who is now my dog,

and I think: How did I end up with this fluffy little creature?

The little white dog lets me know when she needs food,

she pulls me around the neighborhood.

I pick up her droppings like a stooge.

She barks at the other dogs,

but makes friends with the humans.

I do the opposite.

Before I met my wife I was so drunk all the time I couldn't keep a pet.

In AA they advise that before you try a relationship with a person to

try a pet. Or, in bad cases try a houseplant, and see if you water it.

I did one better: I bought a plastic plant that didn't need water.

It had solar panels and sat in the window waving when the sun hit it.

But then I got drunk, fell down, and broke the fucking thing.

Then my wife picked me up.

She taught me how to love again.

She had this little dog, and we treated it like a baby.

I never had a dog, even as a boy in Wisconsin.

I never loved an animal so much.

Soon, I began to love myself again.

Before she rescued me, my wife rescued the little dog from the pound.
That dog used to roam the streets in a gang.
It ate garbage. It had other owners, but ran away.
It shivered in thunderstorms and fought other dogs.
So now she doesn't trust her own kind, and barks at dogs.
Just as I know people are dogs… It's hard to trust.

The dog and I are friends.
The dog and I are the same.
We are both lucky to be adopted by my wife.
We are tramps, mutts, bums…
We both love my wife.
We both make good pets,
as long as we are fed.

The Silent Auction

       Through the folded walls in my mind,
across neighborhoods,
reconstructed cities,
forgotten days,
oozes the color of time:
       rusted sunsets
       green dripping faucets
       beige crumbling wallpaper
       the last gasps of the twentieth century
       a box in a basement with a
       heart shaped diamond where a ghost makes his prison.

It starts as soon as you are born:
       a baby cries,
       a baby screams.
They will hush you,
they will place you in a glass cube.
       Girls must be quiet, graceful, and beautiful.
       Boys must be strong, silent, and hard.

At school
you must raise your hand to talk.
       It's an assembly line,
       an invisible conveyor belt.
We are livestock
       for factories and wars, offices and street sweeping
       for smiles on Christmas Cards.

Muted
Muzzled

Silenced
Sold
Daydreams and nightmares, routines and car accidents

 No one wants to hear your problems.
 No one wants to hear your dreams either.
 You could have the meaning of life wrapped up,
 and no one would care unless there was a price tag on it;
 not to buy it as much as to resell it.

Sold out
Burnt out
Broke down
Blitzed
Mum like an atheist at an AA meeting

 Small talk as interesting as the wind,
 the boss wants yes men,
 the wife is sick of your old stories,
 and your friends think they know you better than you know
yourself.
 Like a worn out joke,
 it was funny—now, it's just true.

And all the things we plug our aching mouths with:
pacifiers and candy
cigarettes and joints
junk-food and tits
kisses after an argument
phalluses and toes
thumbs and bottles
all to fill the void, to hush the voices within.

Clichés roll in our jaws from an invisible ventriloquist.
Old expressions fall out our lips like cud.

>All the music is growing softer.
>The great films are fading.
>Memory is dissolving like burning leaves.
>I remember us wild boys and our smart-cracking mouths,
>now silenced with drugs, paranoia, work, and exhaustion.
>Broke at last, now that we have money…

But we must keep getting out there,
have to be social.
Everything starts the same: Where you from? Where did you go to
school? What do you do to make money? And don't you love your job?
Any answer leads to a list of assumptions as if these things define who
we are.
All parrot talk. All Karaoke.
Or worse, they always ask about sports. I either pretend an interest or
tell them the truth: I don't follow sports. See their faces slowly sag and
their eyes fade. The world could be ending or the house on fire, and
people would still be watching sports.

>Well here's what I do, since you asked:
>I'm hired to read a script to pissed-off customers in a call
center.
>I'm wired up to the whole country.
>Every state has its own brand of redneck.
>All work and no play inspires me to write clichés like: "All work
and no play."
>I'm losing my voice as a writer.
>I'm literally losing my voice talking on the phone all day.
>Losing my voice screaming it out raw at night.

Shivering up my spine runs
drunken flashbacks,
repressed embarrassment,
all my misplaced words play on repeat forever,
pictures of angel-fangs
flashing at orgasm,
echoes of children teaching each other the same
dirty rhymes every generation forever.
A tidal wave of vaporized moments push time forward.
Skeletons march animated by the sun.
Hear the sizzle of heartbeat rhythms:
      rumors, fantasies, parables
      superstitions, ghetto wisdom, backwoods witchcraft,
      jingles, ancient codes encrypted in farts,
      death-wishes cooking in flesh.

      Approaching middle age
I'm starting to go with it.
I lean into the silence.
"If you can't say anything nice don't say anything at all."
I don't want to hear the world either.
I am flattened.
      I think: what is the point in saying anything?
      All echoes in the void…
Words have meanings, then double meanings, then more.
It's all taken wrong.
If it isn't buzzwords, fear mongering, or cult-like positivity the words
are ignored.
      If the world doesn't want to hear what I have to say then that is
the world's loss.
I'm strong and silent at last.

Nightmare: An auction house. The auctioneer is hairless. He wears a
tuxedo with a red bowtie. He has scar tissue like a burn victim. His
mouth is sealed over. The people in the audience raise their paddles to
bid. I cannot see over the shoulders at what is being sold.

　　　But it's a new day!
Wake up America, and smell the garbage islands.
The orchestra churns silently in our pulse.
Time goes by as fast as it always has, only our perception seems to
speed it up.
Desensitized to the days slipping by, just trying to get each miracle
over with.
The mirror is in fast forward.
The great red spot of Jupiter winks.
The average height of a person is going up.
They are keeping teeth on necklaces.
Bootlegs of silence sell on street corners.
People in shadows make love to the sound of
whales humming the apocalypse.

　　　For some religion gives absolution.
　　　When god has all the answers,
　　　they leave life up to him and stop questioning.
　　　Then vows of silence,
　　　meditation,
　　　middle paths,
　　　shrugs beyond opinions.

　　　But it's a new world!
There is nowhere left to explore
except outer space, and inner space.

Off to the races!
America: the middle of everywhere,
    the frontlines of nowhere,
    orgies of the heartland hum like static on
my corporate phone.
    This tower of babel
begins to sound like white-noise,
    like a bell that never rang,
    like before the big bang,
    like the sun forgotten,
    like peace at last,
    like perfect silence
        sold.

My Wife Combing Her Hair Brings Me Peace

Eyes
in the dark woods
meet and grow tender.
Soft footsteps behind me,
then her hand in mine.
She is the only one in the wilderness.
She keeps me warm when cold,
hopeful when my demons descend.

There is so much pain in the world,
but together we are strong.
I tease her.
She rolls her eyes at me.
We laugh,
we cry,
like damp birds in a nest,
we sleep.

Sleeping by the Seine

A sea of souls flutters just under the surface of night.
Silhouettes flicker in rolling waves like a mad carnival ride.
A whirling film of overlapping scenes of someone else's dreams.
Flying buttresses of lunging demons torpedo to oblivion.
Who woke these webs of beards & boney branches like flayed polytheist
saints?

Two thousand years of spiritual graffiti ooze in streetlights & flashbulbs
in the skull.
Obscene caricatures of the heart boil in Buddha-belly cauldrons.
Numb inertia of a long occupied continent gasps & gurgles.
Whispers run down the gutter thirsty for more blood & rain.
My fractured selves crumble beneath this ancient ghost dance.

Tourists dissect symbols like meat pies and the super-ego goes cross-eyed.
The flayed center sparks fireflies, big-bang hatchlings, & lipstick on the
mirror.
Where heads once rolled they drag their feet, point, grin, & photograph.
These spoiled beneficiaries of old revolutions are wholesome vampires of
time & toil,
but still just peasants picking paper for an ever receding bottom line.

Bells & sirens hum in the rows of fleeting neon.
Cigarette butts hang in spider webs of sugar.
Woodpeckers tap Morse code as they change the names on graves.
Making love in shadows, in mausoleums, in dioramas stacked to the sky.
On this tectonic I can finally look over my shoulder & read left to right.

Old Book

I read a book from the 1930's,
last printed in the 60's,
it's out of print now,
written by a friend of a friend
of a more famous writer.

Each page I pass
comes undone from the binding,
and crumbles like moth wings between my fingers.
The pieces fall like dried leaves to the floor,
but I go on because the words are bright, bleak, true.

The lines are coded pictures drawn from a man's ribs
who smoked endlessly, skipped dinner with friends
to write this, and died early so he could live free.
Full of himself but full,
never knowing if anyone would care, and sometimes not caring himself,
alone with the gods, careless but carefree.

The women he writes about were promised immortality.
They were preserved for nearly a century, which is better than make-up,
or mirrors, embalming, or faded photos.
Alive and vibrant, hungry and lustful for a hundred years, though
now they are skeletons softer than this paper.

Out from the center, pressed between the pages,
falls a small blue clover.
Not a romantic flower, almost a joke.
A time capsule, a memento with an unknown meaning,
a seed from a distant reader before the book drifted to me.

The book was once new; an investment for some man with a cigar,
fresh and exciting for some kid, a scandal for some church matron.
It journeyed through cafes, libraries, schools, bargain bins, storage
lockers.
It sat for a lifetime unread on a shelf, then given away, almost thrown
in the trash,
until I found it in a box that said: "For Free."

A man's whole life is entombed in this book.
I search his name on a screen where no one seems to care.
As it crumbles between my hands I think, "Perhaps I am the last one
to read this?"
His memory ends with me, and mine with you.
All you can say is *hello*.

Waiting for the Past

The bush pilot spat on the floor. Everyone had to wait for the rains to lift before the plane could leave the village. Meanwhile there were no deliveries in or out.

The whole area was under quarantine, mosquito nets and bandanas, sign language at the market, the smell of rain and jungle rot where life and death swirl in dense circles creating winds and rumors.

They played checkers with empty cans, tuna for black and salmon for red, and listened to the maddening putter of rain on the tin roofs. They fought off cabin fever and dreaded literal symptoms.

Their first date was through gas masks holding hands up at the water tower where the sunset used to be. No chemical attraction to be sure but the pageantry was stimulating enough.

He took her home and set up the projector. Between tents of plastic sheets they lay breathing through their masks. He inserted the electric jack into the back of his neck, which shot his dreams on a screen showing an intermesh of memories and images, and snippets of jokes no one will get for a thousand years.

His arm around her patted her soft shoulder. As they slept the rain fell like piano hammers searching for the heart.

Sirens rose like trumpets announcing the elephants at the gates. Laser language shot fear into the elders. But for the next generation all this doom and gloom will be simply reality and no one will be the wiser of the slow descent to bone on bedrock.

Hangover Prophecy

when all the graves sprout seeds
when knotted eyes are in the trees
when the stars are washed away by cities
when the skulls hatch
& the sun blinks
& the artic tide comes in
all that we've loved and forgotten
will come back to claim us

Part 4 – Pay Per View Apocalypse

Voice to Skull Transmission

Normandie Avenue between Fountain and Santa Monica is a quiet drag in East Hollywood. Here the rent is higher than other parts of the country but not too high for the service industry to have a bed. Those that by day take care of the children of the rich, who run the cafes, the drycleaners, the auto repair shops, those that run the machinery of West Hollywood or Beverly Hills. The help sleeps here at night. After the smog from rush hour settles it glows in that famous California sunset. Mechanics, delivery people, Uber drivers, accountants, customer service, unemployed, disabled vets hang their hats here. But no one wears hats anymore. It's 2020, or is it 2022 already?

Quarantine is in effect. Now those laid off or on furlough are home. Those that are lucky enough to work from home are on the block all the time. No need to leave. Safer to have food delivered. The meat ain't meat. The air is too dirty to open the window. There is a filter on the tap water. No one comes in here except once a month when the exterminator fumigates. Then we wear masks inside as well as out.

On Normandie if you look closely at the line of cars parked along the curb you might notice something strange. Like clockwork just before dinner the men leave their houses and get in their cars. The doors slam. The radios start up. On hot nights some start their engines to run the AC. But none of the cars pull out. No one leaves. The silhouettes behind the glass sit still. Some smoke a cigarette. Some chew candy. Some nurse a six-pack from a plastic sack.

As they sit in cars with nowhere to go the radio is interrupted by sentimental ads about how someday soon we will be able to leave our homes and see each other again. Rub shoulders. Hug. Shake hands. Embrace. The men in the cars know the other side of the story. The pandemic has made their mortgage-boxes crowded. Like floating space stations the houses are full day and night. Full of the kids, wives, pets, and if you were bad in another life the in-laws are there too. There is little reason to leave. When you do leave you're confined by social distancing. Necessary to stop the spread of the virus true, but still confined. People were in the way before but now they are in the way before they even get six feet in front of you. It would be nice to be social again sure, but it would be even nicer to be alone for a few minutes. Now the car is the only sanctuary on the block.

After a couple beers, a few long drags on a smoke, or just some good tunes from the stereo the guys in the cars start to decompress. Soon the windows come down. Some yell across the street. Hey is that you? You still there? How's the wife? How's the kids? Driving you crazy? … Graduating… piano lessons? What's that setting you back? … Don't tell the wife I'm eating candy. Suppose to be off sugar. You know these LA women. All want to live forever… Well, you shoulda married a Scientologist for that shit… Me I hope there is no afterlife at all. One life is enough for me. Keeps things special. No use dragging things out. Wear out your welcome… Hey, if you keep talking like that I'll come over there and cough on you. You'll be eating your words all week wondering if I gave you the Covid. You'll be clinging to sweet life hoping for more time. You'll be making up gods, praying to old ones, and sweating fever dreams about the afterlife.

From our cars we look up at the apartment building on the west side of the street. A mosaic of characters hang in the brick windows: The old lady singing in the shower. The mustached hipster on his phone. The teenager sounding like he is having a mental breakdown. The bald man hacking a lung elbows on the sill sneaking a smoke. The family cooking beans and rice laughing in a chorus. A panorama of people hangs in the air. We have water. We have light. We have entertainment. We have food. We have drink. We have each other. Things could be worse. Things have been worse. Just look at history. But still. Will things ever get better?

Some of the men in the cars wave from behind the glass as I walk my dog. The yards are dioramas: the bunny house with southwest landscaping little Fiats and rabbit cages. The house where the elderly Asian lady keeps thirty-six potted plants in the yard and waters them with one long hose. The little man in the baseball cap sleeping in the grass sometimes wakes up and picks from the orange tree. The elementary school where kids cackle, cry, and traumatize each other. The chop shop where gear-heads clamper day and night. The yard where chickens roam free and roosters trumpet at dawn. The house with remnants of playing cards and empty Coronas strewn on the lawn under the white noise of a ball game from an old transistor radio. Neglected dogs in mop-locks bark at every passer-by. Joseph keeps his grey hair long in honor of his Indian heritage and makes his tenth trip to the corner all day coming back with hot Cheetos and Yoohoo. There's the mullet man yelling at anyone who parks in front of his house as he blares Pearl Jam. The AA meeting in the grass is sipping coffee and cigarettes. The overweight Star Wars fans who never pick up after their giant hound. The stoners on their porch clicking on laptops as they fume purple skunk in the air. The one house where no one lives enclosed in vines and wooden planks. Lime Scooters line the curb. Teens bop to buzzing beats on plastic cells. Sunshine, distant ocean breezes, tropical flowers juxtaposed with the trash only humans can make, desert rats, jungle rot, giant prehistoric insects that know no winter. The street lamp bends like a neon question mark framing a halo around the man in the gutter.

This afternoon the men shuffle out to sit in their cars to find a flyer under each windshield wiper. The white sheet waves in the wind. Another advertisement for shit we don't need? No… It makes for good reading as we loiter in our cars lined up for a drive-in movie that never begins and never ends. It reads:

Are you going to allow your children's bodies and minds to be controlled and repressed remotely by criminals? Research then pass it on. OUR BODIES AND MINDS ARE HACKED AND THEN TORTURED WITH ADVANCED TECHNOLOGY AND VOICE TO SKULL. IT IS DONE REMOTELY AND DIFFICCULT TO PROVE. This torture includes sexual stimulation or control, sleep deprivation, intimidation to participate in harassing others, symptoms are created- then misdiagnosed and medicated for life, thoughts are read, dreams inserted, subliminal messages sent, thoughts erased, the ability to learn or understand is sabotaged, all types of pornography sent, moods and states of being created. With extreme surveillance our lives are recorded, and with our bodies and minds hacked, the worst invasion of our privacy. 90% of the people don't know this torture is inflicted on them, only the ones on voice to skull 24/7 know. THE POLICE AND FBI HAVE BEEN MADE AWARE AND ARE UNWILLING TO HELP US, THEY ARE ASKING FOR EVIDENCE WHICH IS HARD TO OBTAIN OR SENDING US TO THERAPY. THIS IS THE BIGGEST CRIME AGAINST HUMANITY, PERPETRATED BY THE 1% (THE BIGGEST CO. AND INSTITUTIONS). THIS IS NOT SCI-FI OR FAKE NEWS, IT IS REAL, AND I AM ASKING FOR HELP. HELP US START CAMPAIGNING, THEN WE CAN ASK THE GOV. TO INVESTIGATE AND STOP THIS CRIME. Research Voice to Skull, Targeted individuals, rlighthouse.com, pass it on to anyone who might help, we need their attention and cooperation. I CAN'T FIGHT THIS ALONE. Local voice to skull transmission sent from XXXX N. Hobart blvd. L.A. CA.

Curious about the flyer I stroll to the nearby address accused of relaying the transmissions. It's a block off the main drag quiet enough that the alley cats feel comfortable sleeping in the middle of the road. The street light flickers. Crumbling Victorian houses have excess relatives bunking on porches, swinging in hammocks and pulling mattresses out of the dewy lawn. Other houses are fenced in and boarded up, but you can hear people stirring inside whispering as quiet as they can. Coming to the address in question it looks as strange or as normal as the rest. Another mystery never solved. As the last shadow on the West Coast joins the night the Pacific paradise darkens to Bosch. The Sunset Strip glows orange under the streetlights. Junkies limp and stagger like ghosts their drool drips in rainbows under the neon pulse of the Dollar Store sign.

Everyone has anchors of joy. Some point at their hotrod or dissolve into plasma screens that fill the wall saying ain't this the life? These sunglasses are worth more than most sunglasses. Fuck you sunshine. But the more they talk the more they are just talking to themselves, convincing themselves this is it this is it this it… Is it? There's got to be a better world than this right? Or is this world only as good as we make it? We've made a mess of Eden. But it doesn't get any better than the garden no matter what the ads say. The rich reach for space. Phallic rockets ascend the aqualung. But the heavens are full of airless deserts and frozen worlds, gas globes ignited in flame and fuming with poison.

There are parts of L.A. under marshal law where the cops have given up and the rest don't care. Blocks of tent villages… Used toilet paper line the gutter. Human shit and used needles on the sidewalk… You can tell it's not dog droppings. It's sticky, strewn, the kind of shit from eating garbage. Dogs eat better. Shuttered storefronts. Open air drug markets. When it's not a movie the slick noir feeling burns away. This is real. This is live. This is a stage-play where the actors aren't acting just reacting like spiders on a stove. The characters don't know who they are nor do they care. Reality burns in all colors of the spectrum up close and filling the peripheral all at once. It doesn't take long for the fascination to wear off, just endless time and trial. Echoes of death threats, spittle, and fireworks ring in the avenues. Crows cackle clicking codes.

Police helicopters stutter in the sky. Lisping, demanding, chopping up clouds, the spotlight from the chopper peers down on the failed actress missing one shoe who now believes this is her big moment. When that light hits she raises her arms in adulation and begins to dance, sing, recite that Tennessee Williams soliloquy… She's no longer faking it like that screen test… it's real. She's no longer pretending to want it, no longer coaxing yes-yes daddy, but father I have seen the light… She steps into the light. She tap-dances into the tunnel of light. Just as she's about to hit that high note the helicopter flies off. It weaves in and out of the shadows on the strip pouring light on the faded motels. Another 15 minutes up and over… another big break broken.

From the skin to the soul we are the color of rain, streaked in falling stars, neon signs glowing through smog. From the homeless to the moguls in the hills we are fireflies. We are moths burning between the desert and the ocean. Choking on salt. Gasping on dust. Screaming like silent era film stars with the title card missing. The children cry not yet knowing why but they can feel it. The elderly know it but have given up on the power of words because the definitions change every generation. The scene fades with the sun sinking like a stage prop. Will there be another day? Always. Though it seems less and less likely all the time. Give me one more wink, one more flash of sun, and I'll say thank you.

Still Moments

In 2005 my friend Alana and I sat in Times Square all night, drinking forties from the bag, wired on yellow jackets to stay up since we had nowhere to sleep that night.

There in the bull's eye of civilization, we swigged in the median somehow unnoticed in the chaos of the crowd, the screens above creating a digital storm of meaningless ads.

This trophy wife character struck up a conversation with us. She said she was having a fight with her rich husband and had found herself in Times Square.

After she vented, and as gently as possible, we explained to her that in the grand scheme of things her problems didn't matter. She took a long pull from Alana's forty.

In 2007 I visited my hometown in Wisconsin to find it flooded. There was only one road into town still dry. The other three roads were across bridges, which were now underwater.

I found my old friends on a silent island of cement, now empty of traffic. We strolled, pointing at the submerged bridges that we smoked under as kids.

Now my delinquent friends were old enough to hit the bars but rarely did. Bars meant suffering the crowd, hicks, shallow jukebox plays, and questions about sports.

We preferred sharing a bottle at a house, strumming guitars or still moments under the moonlight in soft fields by the river. Now the river was everywhere.

Walls of sandbags lined the perimeter. We jaywalked in the ghost town where the cops once stopped us for little more than looking weird. It drove me to the cities.

Once they locked me up in their jail. A cop with little else to do hunted me. Practically ran me out of town with petty drinking tickets.

Since then I've been in Mexico, New Orleans, and other places where a guy can sip suds outside with no reason to worry, unlike back in the land of the free, God's country.

The rain let up and the pavement sparkled in the afternoon sun. For once hitting the bars seemed like fun. A place at the main intersection was still open.

The Duck Inn was a subterranean hole in the wall with a wooden sign of Donald Duck. You literally had to duck under the door as you went down the steps.

The bartender was glad for business. My old friends laughed with abandon. We had mixed feelings about the town going underwater, but we never had to wait for drinks.

When it would have been rush hour, I went outside and stood in the middle of the intersection at Main and Racine and howled with no one to harass me.

When I got back to Chicago the rains were back in buckets. I got off the Wilson Red Line stop at night, on my way back to my studio apartment.

Coming down the stairs into the old Art Deco lobby, I could see people getting soaked within seconds out in the street. A businessman and I paused, thinking the same thing.

He had a fleece overcoat, and I had my bags fresh from Union Station after the long Greyhound bus ride. It was better to wait in the lobby until it stopped pissing so hard.

An elderly Indian woman with missing teeth wandered in. I'd seen her hanging around the corner before, teetering on the curb, always cackling like a friendly witch.

Her long grey hair dripped. Her ragged T-shirt was wet, showing her sagging breasts. She smiled in spite of herself, not giving a fuck. Her eyes disappeared into her grin.

After some small talk, the businessman and I chipped in. Already soaked, the old woman took our money and ventured out into the streets blurred by the rain.

As promised, she returned with a six-pack of Old Style, and the three of us sat on the steps inside the station, drinking and talking like old friends until the downpour softened.

Mercifully, all the rules of civilization cease when nature steps in. The CTA attendant didn't give us any static while we drank and hid from the heavens.

I fished around in my suitcase and pulled out a dry flannel shirt. When I gave it to the old woman, she wrapped it around herself like a scarf.

It was good to be back in Chicago, where everyone knows life is hard no matter who you are and it's best not to make things any harder.

No Words

Words cannot do her justice.
No-one cannot summarize her leaping mind.
Her curves know no linear lines.
Her eyes see both sides-
>(dissect the words, dissect the definitions of the words
>dissect the words that define the definitions.)

Knots of nerves and crystal visions.
Endless fractal-phantasm of inter-reflected fear and love.

Words will not do her justice.
Where are the love poems for the rooftops?
 "It must be romantic to love a poet," her friend assumes.
Maybe for some, but as a poet herself she knows better.

My poetry is blasphemy.
Blasphemy against mass hallucination.
Blasphemy against the civilized god.
My poetry is lines in the sand.
My poetry is a shadow of ink.
My poetry is a sunspot.
My words are protests against all words.
My words are fallen angels,
cinders of black sheep,
fallen but
free.

But I will not blaspheme against her.
I will not define her with the razor of words.
I will not blaspheme against the silence we hold,
the tranquility, the eternity, the acceptance that spans time.

We do not need to play games or entertain to bond.
Our love is not conditional.
I will not define it.

Words cannot do her justice.
This is where my ambition ends: at the shores of love.
This is where my ego dissolves into humility and openness, acceptance.
I will not write my way into the mirror maze of obvious answers.
Love is a feeling, a way of living. Love is beyond words.

At our wedding we wrote our own vows.
Because we were both writers those gathered together braced for epic poems.
But we got straight to the point: Love.
In my vow I said that there were no words.
I was admitting defeat.
I was surrendering my heart to the light of love.
I bow to her.
I gave her a vow of silence.
We have a secret no one will know.
I am so lucky to have found her.
I will not burst the bubble with the prick of my pen.
There are no magic words that could unlock our spell.
There are no words.

Where the Shadows Dance

sleeping on a cliff
ears to the ground
in a cornucopia of
trees, stones, sea monkeys, purple oysters
a tunnel from the ocean to the sky
a phantom symphony hushed in
a megaphone of surf, static, whispers to the stars
a telescope of dreams from heaven to the tops of
underwater mountains
clouds visit, condense like soft dreams in misty tears, and
erase the world
redwoods hum like ancient alien beings
seeds of time, rings of Saturn burn in a
calendar of wood on this cosmic raft made of
vines, nerves, wires, cracking temples, tectonics, skull caps
gusts, whirlpools, funneled explosions
under the dry blue moon
surf like halved-cabbage-frays
titan waves forced through
stone pinholes filling
lagoons full of thought bubbles
gravity pulls between the sun and Jupiter
beats the planet to warty nothing
what are you stirring?
what are we brewing?
washing ashore and
shooting into the air with tails of fire
as the rocks shape the water, eventually
the water shapes the rocks
nature knows this is no man's land

as the continent falls into the sea
all your art is erosion
pendulums like waves
islands in space
goddess Kali crumbles
the Earth hatches
and the volcanoes blow like pipe organs
the car alarms sound their mating calls
cows break out of the slaughterhouse
now the running of the bulls is stampeding down the freeway
lab rats on super drugs gnaw through bars
monkeys tie down scientists and test lipstick on them
menageries burst and lions stalk pedestrians
zoos invade the supermarket
the Ark has reached the new world

The Art of Revolution and the Revolving of Art

Something must be done to change things but we also have to stop
and document what we do so people will remember what we did
so they will be inspired to change things and not just remember
things because remembering things is just dwelling on the past and
something must be done to change things now so things will be better
later.

    Knowing things isn't enough we have to show that we know
things by doing things so people know, you know? We need to do
things but first think about what we are going to do before doing them,
but not think too long because we must do things now so things are
better later otherwise it would be too late just like it was in the past.

    We need to experience things to make art as well as
make art to show our experiences. We can't spend our whole lives
documenting the past but must get out there and see the present to
express what is happening now to the people in the future when they
look to the past so they are inspired to change things in their "now"
which is our "then," and it is not too late again.

    We must do things to affect minds to inspire
actual bodies to do things to affect other minds to affect other bodies
to get out there and get into other minds to get them out into the
world and out of their isolated minds and affect actions to affect minds
to affect actions to affect minds until we burst past the anxiety of linear
time to when the world has no reason to be hate filled and twisted in
the first place.

And I hope "now" is not too late. I hope the past is not forgotten again. I hope a future is born worth the billion birthing pains, and mutates to a form that cannot curl up in the primitive shadows of the past again. I hope brutality becomes as impossible as a coldblooded ancestor, a distant dinosaur, and police states become caveman exhibits in museums, as irrelevant as a flat Earth, and laughable as the grace of a worm. If our minds aren't made up about that then something must be done.

Snowman

My fourth grade teacher had Lyme disease. She survived, but didn't show up for the first few weeks of school. She made up for it because she was promoted to fifth grade as the year ended. So now my class had her two years in a row.

In the middle of the second year a new kid arrived, Norman. He picked his nose and chewed his fingernails openly in class. Our teacher, Mrs. Reece, publically chastised him for it, calling him disgusting and a baby. Naturally, the kids followed her lead and made fun of him at recess, but when Mrs. Reece found out about this they got in trouble for it. She was a hypocrite.

I remember I did an oral book report about the Stalingrad Siege during World War II. I liked playing army and reading about war. As I read my report to the class I described how the soldiers would eat the plaster out of the walls to fend off starvation. I was scolded by Mrs. Reece because this was considered too shocking for the other kids to hear. I was on the verge of tears. My budding little mind couldn't accept the injustice. I got the information from a book in the school library!

Then one day during the English lesson we were picking out the nouns and proper nouns in a sentence. The word snowman was circled on the board. "Yes of course snowman is not a proper noun, he isn't real." It was true. The snowman had no name in the sentence. It was just a snowman. But something about the word *real* stuck in my throat.

I raised my hand. Mrs. Reece called on me. "A snowman is still real," I said.

"Real? A snowman isn't real. Let's go on."

"No, not alive, but a snow man is still real."

"Westley. Stop being silly." There were snickers from the other kids now.

"Well, he's not a man, but he's still a real thing." More laughs.

"You're being ridiculous! What's got into you?" Now Mrs. Reece was laughing at me.

I had to make myself understood. I struggled for the words but I knew I was right. A snowman was made out of snow and water, and that is real as anything else. The kids laughed because they heard *real* like Frosty the Snowman became real, or Pinocchio became a *real* boy.

"No! Not real like being alive, but real like a rock is real."

"Ok. That's enough!"

"NO! I mean…"

"STOP IT! BE QUIET!" Mrs. Reece pointed her boney finger at me. She was turning red and started shaking. "DON'T YOU RAISE YOUR VOICE AT ME!"

Again, I was in trouble. Again, it wasn't fair. But I didn't feel any tears this time. I sat back, smiled, and said smugly, "Oooo-kay." Her red face looked confused. Her eyes swam around in her head. I was beginning to realize that someday soon I would be smarter than her. The thing about the snowman was just a semantics argument sure, but

I felt soon I would leave her behind on a philosophical level: what was real and what was not.

After teaching us for two long years the last day of school finally came. This time it was Mrs. Reece who cried. She had grown attached to us. She was oblivious to the fact that most of the kids hated her. I couldn't wait for her to stop sniveling. I couldn't wait for the final bell to ring. I couldn't wait for summer to come. I couldn't wait to leave.

The Smile Never Fades from My Skull

I have my pandemic mask on. I have my sunglasses on.
I have earphones on. I have latex gloves on.
I cannot smell or taste. I am blocked from the sun.
I am programming what I hear. I am cleaned, clothed, and
quarantined. I am ready.
(I have dabbled in sensory deprivation tanks before.)
The apartment is our space station filtered through an
air-conditioner, TV monitors, pipes and wires.
Happiness comes from within yet we are all connected.
As the seventh seal unfolds no one cares until it happens to them.
The LA air clears of smog. The Venice canals are cleaned of oil.
The Earth renews as we slow our consumption.
Mankind acts as the memory of time but as the globe boils
maybe we should drift off to sleep for the greater good.
The skull always smiles.
The lips shape life, smile, frown, and pucker.
The lips kiss goodbye and
forgive
forget
regenerate
evolve
escape
into
eternity or
the lack there of
where there
will be no more men alive
no afterlife dragging on
forever.

No more memory
no worries
only silence.
The Earth heals
free from bats
free from doves
free from demons
free from angels
free to be
long
past
the measure
of time.

Keep Your Shirt On

Jason S. was throwing a rent party. When I caught wind of the shindig I showed up early. His place was on the second floor of a walk-up on Milwaukee Avenue just north of Division in Chicago. I was determined to outlast everyone at the party and claim the spot on his sofa for the night. At the time I was on the street. Most of the time I slept on the floor of a warehouse on the West Side. So I took any excuse to crash somewhere else.

First order of business Jason needed some beer otherwise people wouldn't show up. Across the street was a Jewel Osco. Walking with Jason to the liquor section he told me to act casual, which was easy because I had no idea he was about to lift a 30-rack of PBRs right under the noses of the security guards. Jason was always clean-cut, wore nice leather shoes, and a suit-coat over a button up. No one would have ever suspected him.

He hefted the case of beer and walked confidently towards the front door. The touch of genius was that as he walked he produced a receipt from his suit pocket and studied it as he casually strolled towards the exit. Anyone manning the security cameras would have figured he paid for the 30-rack at the register back by the liquor department to avoid the long lines at the front checkout. His receipt was for a 30-case. Only the date was wrong.

Jason's roommates had done their share gathering ice, bottles, and stacks of red cups sold for five bucks to get in. Already inside I drank for free. The crowd smoked on the fire escape, which overlooked the point where the Blue Line plunged underground into the tunnels downtown. Israel and Stephanie showed up after they had played a gig at the Blue Star Lounge. They partied like rock stars and the hours evaporated.

Conversations darted in the usual directions. How Wicker Park was
different when we were still in school. How condos were popping
up and the rent was rising. Hence the desperate rent party. "Just
look at the trendy Sushi restaurant outside the window across the
street." Already Logan Square, the next neighborhood to the west,
was replacing Wicker as the haven for staving artists. Jason said he'd
probably move that way next.

"Should read how Nelson Algren described this neighborhood in *The
Man with The Golden Arm*," I began to bore everyone about a book
written in 1949 but heeled my high horse. "Point is that even these
days will become someone else's glory days. As things supposedly
get better the less they seem like the good old days. It just pushes
everyone further west, and away from the sterile center of The Loop
downtown."

Around three in the morning few people lingered. Empty cups
and cigarette butts were strewn about. Stephanie sat in the corner
strumming a guitar. Jason sat on the windowsill counting the wet bills
checking if they'd make rent. Israel and I scoured the kitchenette on
the other side of the room checking the cabinets and the crisper for
any more refreshments. "Dude," said Israel. "I think we're tapped out
and everything is closed."

Jason looked out the window. "The Sushi place is still open. They
have a bar with an after hours license if you guys want a nightcap."
The four of us put on our coats and let gravity guide us down the
stairs. As we approached the door of the Sushi place two young guys
came out, turned around, and appeared to be locking the place up
for the night. They had their aprons slung over their shoulders. They
must have been the chefs.

"Don't close up yet," said Israel. "Let us come in for one more." The chefs smiled but said they were closed. Israel persisted. "Come on guys. Let's hang out. I'll tip big." The chefs were healthy young men, but had obviously put in a long night's work. I knew it was useless so I slumped my frame across the hood of the little hotrod parked at the curb waiting for Israel to tire himself out. I closed my eyes maybe to take a little nap.

Jason sparked a cigarette. Stephanie scratched her head. Her whole scalp moved showing that her crown of blue locks was really a rock and roll wig. The chefs inched past Israel and began unlocking the car I happened to be laying across. The sound of the keys in the door made my eyes pop open. They smiled at me. The driver pointed, said something in Japanese, and the other laughed. "Hey guys. At least give me a ride." They seemed game.

Still grinning the driver strapped in and revved up the engine. I gripped the edge of the hood where the wipers came out still smiling through the windshield. When he hit the gas the car gunned up Milwaukee Avenue at full speed. Wide-awake now I clung to the hood. My legs dangled a bit as I laughed into the windshield. The chefs were laughing too. After hitting the high gear the driver cut the engine and pulled over to the curb.

Gently I slid off and said, "Whoa, what a rush!" Truth be told this wasn't my first time car surfing. It was a pastime growing up back in hicksville Wisconsin. But my new friends didn't seem to sense this. They weren't smiling anymore. The driver had exited the vehicle and now he was bouncing on his heels like he wanted to box. I suppose he had hoped to scare me off but was disappointed when he saw I had a death wish.

As he came closer he pulled his shirt off revealing his carefully sculpted pecks and abs. The guy was small in stature but desperately tried to make up for it by bodybuilding. Me being six foot and burly I had long since wasted what nature had bestowed upon me. I laughed again and rubbed my beer belly as I told him, "You know you could beat me up with your shirt on. This ain't a movie."

As I stood there grinning he landed a right hook in my big dumb jaw. I was numb from the drinks and the cold. It tickled like a leg asleep. I could have just fallen on the guy and ended the fight, but just then Stephanie and Israel caught up with us. Stephanie screamed a streak as blue as her hair. When she slapped the chef on the shoulder her wig fell off. Israel picked up the wig for her and dragged me away. "Go work out," I told the driver.

At Jason's we helped clean up. I got my sofa for the night. Israel and Stephanie made a bed on the floor. The next day I felt bad for the miscommunication with our neighbors. Telling Jason the rest of the story as he found us blankets he just shook his head and said maybe it was time for him and his roommates to move. It's cheaper out west, and the rent party had come up short. I gave him the five bucks I owed for a red cup.

Pay Per View Apocalypse

Inky stickmen collide, battle, bleed in childhood war-games. Chemical-burn on Polaroids shift over family faces in time-blur. Selfish as Satan we burn ants in the sun with a Godlike magnifying glass. Locking horns with hunger. Hearts going cold as the Earth heats up. Digital mirages splash in fickle fun. Plastic oceans ripple like a blue tarp over a homeless encampment. Sea levels rise and fresh water sold in bottles make more plastic for the ocean, micro-dosing fish and ourselves. They say we drink it too. Not a turtle with a straw through its nose yet, but soon we will be plastic automatons gasping like fish.

The sun swarms like a fleshy octopus. Mars steps forward and icecaps melt the red desert into Earth. Earth falls forward into the greenhouse effect like sulfuric Venus. Humans dig deeper underground air-conditioning vents like snorkels to the surface inhale oxygen and spew out poison. Only Jupiter holds our weight from falling into the sun. Kali dances on the pyre. In the name of Jesus we kill nature, when nature is God. We eat our mother from inside the womb, umbilical cord out into space. Nature gave birth to man. Man gave birth to the machines. Long after our flesh suffocates the mechanical children will spin like tops mining minerals to make themselves. A laser-eye sees God, winks.

Oxy-morons like "corporate-culture" shake hands in the Freedom Tower. Wal-mart greeter says hello coming in. On the way out asks, "Why would you ever leave Wal-Mart?" Dollar bills stapled to the forehead. Slave songs echo from Egypt to Globalization. Domestic addiction, routines spiral to extinction. George W. Bush is off the whisky and coke, now painting puppies. X marks the spot where JFK was shot. You can put your head through a cutout in the Book Depository and pose. A picture of a picture. A copy of a copy. A selfie of suicide. God masturbates in the mirror. The Last Supper is one sided.

Smile. Blow out the candles. Pose for a freeze-dried drop of time.
Once more around the sun. Parodies of ourselves. Masks of glass.
Cameos in our own lives. Selfies in civil war. Let's pretend to be
individuals. Now let's pretend to be one. Shadow boxing with the void.
Too drunk to know the dawn from the dusk. Antimatter shakes the
sky. Demon violins sew the fate of the Milky Way. Don't you know the
Big Bang was God's death? Now Eternity spins in slow motion. God
created evolution and we'll evolve into God. Just as likely, once we
fully come to power we'll blow ourselves up, like the Big Bang again.
The cycle continues, a universe within a universe like Russian dolls,
stillborn, eternal.

Cartoon devils dance in my head. We voted for the Beast.
Hallucinogenic smog frames the sun unseen as we're inside watching
mass manifestation via streaming service. Selfish as sin I'm an agnostic
using mystic symbols for shorthand for the shadows inside. Straddling
the fence as both sides burn: one in effigy, one in denial. Without the
spine to be a modern man I crave cannibalism to take on the strength
of my enemies. Meanwhile sipping molten pennies bidding my time
under the amber sky just writing poems about the apocalypse. Seeking
immortality when we only plan one generation at a time. The horizon
hits the windshield. The veins in my wings burst. The flag unfurls
spread-eagle.

The urgency of now diluted in cosmic soup. Geologic time looms
like the voices of the dead drawing us to dinosaur graves, the next
sediment of the dusty pages of Earth, a line in the tree, a star in
the apple. TV waves radiate into the void like a death rattle, signal
un-received, mute as a silent movie star mouthing the words.
Counterculture is green-washed by cold shower classrooms. Open
road, open questions. Open mind, no convictions. Ends endless.

Means meaningless. Imprisoned in quotations. Universe implodes in galactic cobwebs like neurons severing. Inner space erased. Talking tumors whisper a kaleidoscope of sarcasm. Control fetishes echo in the church of the skull.

A malaise of oneness. A drone of synchronicity. Wallpaper peels to reveal the effects of suburban geometry on the psyche. The lab-rat won't run the maze any more. Alaskan Cruise Ships take the ice from the melting glaciers and make Margaritas. Voices of warning reduced to art. Voices of doom reduced to street corner prophets holding cardboard signs. Revolution reduced to teenage poetry as ineffective as 666 in a spiral notebook. Drums echo in abandoned buildings. Paint the walls black for my dead twin. I put pins in myself to feel him. We play chicken in the street. Mixed metaphors drank straight. Truth slurred in surrealism. Death bounces in like a fool with bells on.

Hollywood Ending

After some fucked up street shit happened
again.
It was enough to make me paranoid enough
to ask:
Perhaps if I stop writing about fucked up
street shit
maybe fucked up street shit will stop
happening?

If intention is real, then I will write it:

He was loved. His wife was loved. They loved each other. They
worked on their dreams and were rewarded. He and his wife made
love, didn't want for anything, and grew to know each other's souls
throughout the years more and more. They became known for their
words so much that they no longer needed day jobs. They could
take vacations when they wanted. They traveled the world. As they
traveled they saw the world change, adapt, transition to clean energy
--- scientifically and spiritually. The environment rejuvenated. The
Earth healed. The people evolved. The countries and cultures ceased
to clash. There was a great awakening. There was a global golden age.
There was a great new beginning. The end.

The Agnostic at AA

There is always reason.
There is always a reason
to do what you want
even when you don't want to.
To do what thou wilt.
Wilting to what you do.

There are always two sides.
There are usually more.
There is a sip between wisdom and
delirium.
There is so much that can't be proved.
There is so much that can't be disproved.
There is so much to be known.
There is so much beyond human knowledge.
There is a thin line.
There are no lines.
There is a space between.
There is a thin line between artistic inspiration,
mystic revelation, and madness.
The lines are blurry, beautiful, a quasi riddle where
dreams are more real than reason
a sad joke
a punch line
a line between
within and
without
where subjectivity and
objectivity are just words.

There are no sides for the Buddha.
There's one side for the Individualist.
Two sides for the fire & brimstone preacher.
Three sides in the Trinity.
Four corners of the world for those still seeking.
Five points to a pentacle.
A labyrinth of shapes beyond.
An infinite Tesseract in the Kabala.
Circles in philosophy.
Scales tip and totter
peacefully impartial.
All tranquility in the void.

Nothing beats the feeling of living & knowing what you know.
Though no one really knows what you know
for no one has lived what you have lived.

There is too much
seeing but not looking
hearing but not listening
touching but not feeling
looking but not seeing
listening but not hearing
feeling but not touching.
See what I did there?
If not that's okay too.

Silent words. Loud pictures.
Colorful music.
A menu of synesthesia
for the agnostic omnivore

harmonious hermaphrodite
ambidextrous dyslexic
androgynous genius
well-rounded hypocrites
chasing tails like
Ouroboros round the sun
ever hungry
at the cusp of harvest
on the fence
on the wagon
mind open
heart exposed
closing in on the light
at the end
of the tunnel of time
telescoping back to
the crystal mirror
the reflecting eye
sight unseen
arms crossed
arms on the cross
legs crossed
on the lotus
heart exposed
beating broken
but keeping time
all the time
all

Ghost in the Graveyard

before alcohol
before sex
before drugs
the rotary phone
would ring
& we would meet outside
in the dark
until our eyes
would absorb
the moonlight
& the glow of the
distant towns
reflecting halos upon
the clouds.

We would run
chase
make up games
exhilarated only
by the heart racing
the thrill of being
young and our
whole lives ahead
endless,
formless,
because they were
limitless
timeless.

Tag, you're it.
You're always it.
In barns, in pastures,
between gravestones,
beyond white tombs,
beyond white roads,
dipping in the swimming hole
molded in brown syrup.

Playing hide and seek
when found
we would
kiss
and feel
excited
confused
the heart
full of pangs
knowing we didn't
love each other &
during the day we
didn't even like each other
but were in love
with our childhood
that was so quickly
slipping away
& we only felt it
when we'd close our eyes
pretend
& make up memories for later
for never
for now.

Illuminated

What's kept private
will haunt you.
What's made public
will haunt you.
You
haunt yourself.
You
possess yourself
like a sock puppet
where
the hand of god
is
up the esophagus
whispering
the past
& feeding the future
like a
baby bird
nibbling the present
learning to fly.

I vent.
I confess.
I prophesize.
I scream.
I tag the air.
I dance like a skywriter.
I cry.
I laugh.
I don't know the difference…

It's
exhaust.
I'm
exhausted.
All steam & dreams…
smoke pillars to the sky.
Thoughts hold up the heavens.

But, I know
it's going to be okay.
I don't know where it comes from,
but I have faith…
in the law of averages,
the odds of evens,
in oneness, in
stalemate-statuesque,
even-infinity, the
mean-mean, the
well-well, the
here-here, & the
there-there.
Well-well, &
farewell,
to meet the maker
to make the meter
to measure
time.

You know,
I am the bad guy in the life story of some people.
I am the demon in the memory of some people who used to love me.
This is what makes me try to be kind to everyone I meet now.

God's Small Talk

Wind whistles through a crack in the mountain
drawing the Nile North like the pungi of a snake charmer.
Clouds fume thoughts and rain ideas.
Plants crack rocks to sand, to beach, to desert, to dust.
A trillion shadows bubble on the surface of the Earth.
They form and transform sculpting the arc of time.
Will the end have an audience? Create one?
Is there an end at all? All that is never ends, but
changes, shape shifts, borrows energy, endless.

But we end. That concerns us. Death creates all the stories,
all the tales with a beginning and end. Plot arches like contorted spines.
So much drama, tragedy, comedy to justify our mortality.
The birds do not laugh. The fireflies never cry.
We personify the world with tales of Armageddon.
The true meaning of apocalypse is change not the end.
Even if we choke ourselves burning factories like cigarettes,
the world will go on in some form on and on ever changing.
Even if history is wiped clear there is no wasted time in eternity.

Ever Ever Land

In the future, in
Ever Ever Land,
the code is cracked
the human genome is altered and
the body no longer dies, but
plateaus at 25.
After the last mortal generation
fades over the horizon a
new mood falls over the Earth.
In Ever Ever Land
no one is in a rush.
There's no rush to learn.
There's no need to cling.
Nothing is vital.
Nothing is final.
There is no finale.
In Ever Ever Land
there is nothing but time.

Soon the population piles up.
People are being born but no one is bowing out.
The human race reaches 20 billion.
The Earth is straddled with waste and squeezed for room.
The animals and plants dwindle.
There is not enough food.
Still, no humans die.
The stomachs turn to stone
absorbing energy directly from the sun, but
with a constant headache.

Still, we are running out of space.
Soon there are restrictions on how many
children a parent can have.
Then there are restrictions on sex itself.
No worries. Again there is little to cling to.
With infinite moments few moments are special.
With all the time in the world, there
is no time worth measuring.
Effectively there is little reason to think about time at all.

In Ever Ever Land
the first 100 years are easy.
After 200 years some feel strange.
First, there is too much to know.
Then, nothing left to learn.
Even new things are the same in a way.
Life begins to go round and round.
By 300 there are too many memories,
too many heartbreaks,
too many people who have moved away,
too many people who won't leave, but
keep coming around in circles, cycles,
the same problems and the same answers.
There are too many ups and downs,
so many pangs of regret,
a sea of nostalgia forms too deep to bare.
By 400, in Ever Ever Land,
most go utterly insane.

Legends form around death.
Tall tales circulate about heroes of old who
sacrificed their lives for ideas, for freedom,

who died bravely, who did more in less time
than any of us did with all the time in the world.
The Reaper becomes an underground symbol.
He pops up in graffiti, t-shirts, memes.
The skull becomes an icon deemed: Ole Smiley.

An international business emerges: the Incinerators.
Though the body won't die on it's own
it can still be broke down in a pyre.
By appointment one can bow out with dignity.
First a sedative is administered. Then the body is cremated.
New religions form around the act.
Elaborate funerals that last days are held like mini festivals
where friends and family say goodbye, make amends,
and feast before the Viking funeral.

In response upper echelons in the government begin
promoting the "Digitalization of the Soul."
They recognize the problems the physical body
imposes on the environment.
They see the strain immortality has on the brain.
In droves people abandon their bodies and upload
their consciousness to the web to be preserved eternally.
(That is as long as no one unplugs the grid and the backup
generators don't fizzle out.)
Are you the same person when uploaded?
Is that still your mind?
Does your mind learn in the same way?
Does it change the same? Make decisions the same?
No one really knows…
The faithful who huddle around the Incinerators say no. It is not the
same.

The government argues that the digitized self
may not be exactly the same, but is actually better!
Only the best self is presented online.
Personalities dance with the algorithm, "like" and comment in circles.
However, after only a few decades of digital dreams the electric mind
succumbs to the same symptoms as the aging brain made of flesh.
There are too many memories.
There is too much information.
There are too many sides to consider.
In a sort of grinning insanity the digital minds
become parodies of themselves.
They speak in a jumble of mixed metaphors.
They become a meme of a faded memory.
They are no longer people, but personas.

In Ever Ever Land
we always imagined ever lasting life
would be like Heaven.
Perhaps ever lasting life is more like
an eternal Hell.

You know… if we merely look…
Life is beautiful.
The Earth is beautiful.
Who are we to ask for more?
Maybe it doesn't get any better
than right here, right now.
Heaven is already here.

I Am the Earth

I am the Earth.
I am the dirt, the mud,
the green vegetation that spurned the atmosphere,
the rain that streaks the sky.
I am the hard-on greeting the sunrise,
the worm rebelling against gravity to stand erect against entropy
like a pathetic sundial proclaiming time when really it's eternity.
I am life
basking in light,
spinning, exhaling dreams in the night.

I am the Earth.
I am not Venus or Mars or
Cassiopeia or some other lifeless place where
we assign our myths.
I am life, real life.
I am the mud, the shit.
I am decay.
I am fertility.
I am broken bones.
I am the bloody marrow in the western sky.

I am the Earth.
I am dying.
My receding hairline is the Polar Icecaps melting.
My beer belly is full of garbage islands and nuclear waste.
The cycles under my eyes are the Earth's Magnetic Field worn
by sun-flares, gamma rays, burning spotlight revelations.
My shoulders are Atlas realizing he's just a symbol.
My heart is aching from Christ being misquoted.

My brain is Buddha stuffed in the skull of a fortune cookie.

My blood is dinosaur-bones liquefied into gas prices and pollution.

I can live on sunlight alone but choose to smoke my butt to the filter.

My lungs are wings trapped in the chrysalis of unborn human potential.

I am the Earth.

I am the blue pearl.

I am all the blue words.

I am the cunt, the red flower, the bed of life, rusty sap, and bleeding rivers.

I am the pink scar that heals the wounds of the world.

The cunt that takes a pounding, stronger than anything but called weak, called a pussy.

I am the cunt, blood goddess Kali the creator and destroyer of worlds-your choice.

I am the cunt. I am the living god, but I have cut the cord so you can create your own world, your own incarnation. Good luck.

I am the Earth.

I am the blue sky.

I am all the blue words.

I am man. I am the man. I am a dick, a prod, a probe, a sword, a mushroom cloud.

I must be strong because no one wants to hear my pain.

I must be brave because no one wants to know I am scared.

I kill to survive. I die in order to live.

I will gladly fight wars to defend my homeland.

But, just as often I will also fight wars for no good reason at all.

I am a slave to freedom.

I freed the slaves.

I liberated the death camps of WW2.

I stared horror in the face because I am a man.

I didn't tell anyone about it because I am a man.

I lost my soul, lost my innocence for truth, for justice, so the next generations could stay childlike forever.

I did all the work, and I took all the blame.

I am the Earth.

I am the blue marble.

I am all the blue words.

I am the fag, the fop, the dandy who writes little poems.

I am the darling folk singer meowing around the campfire,

who paints sentimental pictures, and makes black and white movies.

I am the bitch, the beautiful boy with long hippie hair who found

himself in jail being eyed by skinheads, rapists for your prison punch-

lines.

But I kept them at bay convincing them I was crazy until I was.

I am the art-class clown who refused to get undressed in the locker

room with the other boys because of the indignity of it all.

And while the jocks played football and showered together I was the

fag off fucking their girlfriends behind the bleachers, but with me the

cheerleader actually came.

I am the Earth.

I am the blues.

I am all the blue words.

I am a bluesman. I don't believe any white-bred bullshit. I don't suffer fools lightly. I know the American dream is a dream, not reality. I moan at midnight.

I am the heartbeat of the mother continent. I am somehow the outcast yet who is the original man, the origin of culture, the outsider tasked with guarding the sacred flame.

I am the scapegoat. Like Patti Smith sang I am a Rock and Roll Niger. Rock and Roll black sheep by choice perhaps, but sometimes I wonder if there was a choice.

Yeah, maybe I'll never fully understand. But I'm trying. Yeah, maybe I started as a tourist in hell, but now there ain't no going back home. Though I grew up in country-ass heaven I am no white savior. I'm only the Earth.

I am the Earth.

I am the blue eyes.

I am all the blue words.

I am the Nazi. I think I'm better than my fellow man. I think I am better than all the trust fund babies who never worked a day in food service, on a farm, or on the street. I think that I am better than all the academics who never lived a day in their lives. I think I am better than all the rednecks who where fooled by Donald Trump. I think I am better than all the real Nazi's who came out of the woodwork like torch-toting sheep. You see I have good self-esteem. All my flaws are really my quirks. All my mistakes are really adventures. All my character flaws give me character. All my hardships are my strengths… You see the stories I tell myself? You see the games I play? I am better, better, the best… as I kill myself with booze, with carbon dioxide, with mirrors. Really, I hate myself. I am worthless. I am no better than anyone. I can't figure out life alone. I can't figure out love. All I have is my witty hate. I hate society. I hate myself. But I am the Earth. I have absorbed it all. I have survived worse.

I am the Earth.

I am blue balls.

I am all the blue words.

I am the ass. I am laughing, talking shit, the stubborn hee-haw jackass, the third eye of enlightenment winking because I am really the brown eye of bullshit, a bloodthirsty clown, a parody of myself, a scarecrow crucified and stuffed with existential emptiness.

I am the fuck. I am a fuck, a fleeting pulse of adrenaline. I am a cock, a weapon of love. I am violence *and* love. I am anxiety, anticipation, relief… I am orgasmic euthanasia. I am the tender ticking time bomb holding back my load, politely thinking of awful things to keep me from coming before you come. No not baseball, but war footage, the most embarrassing moments, the cringe moments of childhood, like farting in class and getting caught. As we make love all the worst moments are overlaid in my mind with the best moments. Can't get too excited. Can't enjoy things too much. It's a balance. You see I might be a fuck. But I'm a gentleman. Ladies cum first. I am the Earth.

I am the Earth.

I am the blue ice.

I am all the blue words.

I am the devil. I am the fallen angel. A cinder from heaven marooned on Earth. Cast from the womb where all needs were met by a warm God now set free to fend for one's self like a lizard. I slither in this green Eden eating, shitting, until it is my turn to be eaten. The garden eats its tail forever. Lucifer banished to Earth I punish all the sinners for God. In the great machine I do all the dirty work. I absorb all the blame. I am the wrath of God hidden in an animal mask. I am a goat. I am the scapegoat, the sacrificed kid. By definition everything is God. We are all children of creation. Even me the devil. I shovel the shit that fertilizes the crops. I breathe in the sulfur of the egg of life. The legitimate son, the claimed son of God dies for all the sins. Meanwhile I am doomed to live forever doing all the dirty work. Suffering in pain to fulfill the wrath of God… Does this sound like bullshit? Does this sound like myth? Yes, of course. Now you're getting it. Yeah sure, I am the boogieman shaming little kids to be nice before Christmas. And where is God? God, you are the universe. You are long asleep, cold, exploded long ago. All we have is the Earth. All we have is this Eden, this green heaven. All we have is each other. We must save ourselves. We must save each other. All we have is love. It comes from within not from above. Love.

I am the Earth.

I am soil, wind, water, the lightning of life.

I am not Venus or Mars or any other lifeless place we assign myths and symbols.

I am life, real life.

I am dying.

I am gasping.

I am a jokester, a shape shifter sure. But I tell you this: nature is God. God is nature, and man is killing nature. Man is killing God. By assuming there's another world we're killing this world. We're not becoming the angels of our imaginations but demons in reality.

I am the Earth.

I am decay.

I am fertility.

I will bring you life if you help me live.

I am the Earth.

My receding hairline is the Polar Icecaps melting.

My beer belly is full of garbage islands and nuclear waste.

My heart is Christ misquoted.

My lungs are wings trapped in the chrysalis of unborn human potential.

I am the Earth.

About the Author

Westley Heine has tried hard not to be a poet. Yet he is a poet. In the early 2000s he was a painter. But soon words began to dance across the canvas, collaged and crystalized in dense webs of symbolic poetry.

Then he studied film in Chicago aspiring to the larger bullhorn of media. But Heine began creating experimental videos full of dreamlike images. Collaborating with artist Israel Alpizar they made *The Trail of Quetzalcoatl,* a cinema-verite exploration of the Mayan Prophecies. In an attempt to narrate this deluge of psychedelic visions Heine lent his voice to the soundtrack reading his poetry aloud. So alas the road to cinema with any mainstream intent was cast away.

Out of *The Trail of Quetzalcoatl* came Heine's first published volume
of poetry of the same name. Again this was not straight poetry, but
poetry supplemented by photo collage and drawings with the text
weaving between images.

Continuing with spoken-word Heine teamed up with punk
poet and performance artist Sid Yiddish in 2007 to create Two-$-
Cockroach bringing poetry directly to the public. A revolving troupe
of minstrels, including Daniel Stine and Guitar Mike, accompanied
the two poets on their performances across the Midwest peaking with
a featured performance at the original Poetry Slam at The Green Mill.
At this point Heine was close to becoming a practicing poet.

However, having played in heavy metal groups when he was
young, he became tempted to transform the poetry troupe into a
full-fledged band. Influenced by Delta blues and hard-rock Heine
and Guitar Mike formed Cousin Bones. For a period of five years,
and with four albums worth of original demos, the band played most
every club in Chicago, and toured to Brooklyn and the West Village in
New York City. Cousin Bones had various incarnations from a five-
piece group to Heine carrying on the project as a solo artist during
the height of the recession living as a street musician and a squatter.
Deemed the blues poet Heine eventually wondered how much his
words were being lost behind his growling vocal delivery.

After years of being broke and in bad relationships Heine
found himself in a studio apartment in the Albany Park neighborhood
of Chicago. There he lived on whiskey, sold plasma, and occasionally
stumbled to the all night diner down the block. At this point he began
assembling his writing into a series of novels. The stories contained
adventures of youthful exhilaration, but also confessional pieces full
of gallows humor verging on a drawn out suicide note. Luckily Heine
met his future wife and poet Andrea Shoup at the Poetry and Absinthe
reading at Exit, the renowned punk rock club. The couple moved
to Texas, then Hollywood, and traveled to New Orleans and Paris.

Heine continues to write books and mix words and music with various groups including Yogic Drone Technicians, Radio Obscura, and a series of records under the name Heaven's Headache.

Westley Heine has tried hard not to be a poet. Yet he is a poet. Poetry means a life of sure obscurity, little money, and not being understood by the populace at large. It is not a life many people choose. Poetry chooses you. *Street Corner Spirits* contains a variety of pieces published and unpublished over the poet's life. The first section deals with growing up in a small town. The material in the second part comes from living in cities as a young man. Part three deals with coming to terms with mortality. The final section contains recent works written in Hollywood in the wake of the global pandemic. He now resides in Chicago.

Heine's multi-media approach to poetry and all things poetic will likely not dwindle. Yet *Street Corner Spirits* contains raw prose poems, flash fiction, and the purest collection of poetry he has released. Author of *12 Chicago Cabbies* and *Busking Blues: Recollections of a Street Musician & Squatter*, Heine offers a unique look at American life examining love, death, madness, street life, classism, and subculture using his macabre yet sympathetic style.

Acknowledgements

Some of the poems included in this collection were previously published in the following publications. Roadside Press wishes to acknowledge them for their fine work and dedication to the small press.

"Peach Schnapps" and "A Hermit in the City" were previously published in *Bleached Butterfly June 2019*

"My Dog" was previously published in *Verse in Silence 2019 Winter Edition*

"Old Book" was previously published in *Gravitas Volume 19 Issue 1*

"Hangover Prophecy" was previously published in *Wellington Street Review 2nd Edition*

"Just a Bar" was previously published in *Heroin Love Songs Issue X*

"Sugar Skull" and "Sleeping by the Seine" were previously published in the first edition of *Bloom* from Red Penguin Books

"Sugar Skull" and "Plasma Deluge" were spoken word pieces on the album *Sugar Skull* by The Yogic Drone Technicians Featuring Westley Heine

"Cubicle Matthew" and "A Hermit in the City" were spoken word tracks on the album *Misanthropy Monologues* by Radio Obscura

"Karaoke" was previously published in *Dear Booze*

"Still Moments" was previous published in *Brazos River Review April 2022*

"The Art of Revolution and the Revolving of Art" was previously published in *Buk 100 Notes For A Dirty Old Birthday* from Newington Blue Press

"The Smile Never Fades from My Skull," "Bomb," "Digital World," "Waiting for the Past," and "Voice to Skull Transmission" were previously published in the *2022 World on Fire* anthology from Dumpster Fire Press

"Rain Dance" and "Scarecrow Joe" were previously published in *Gasconade Review 8*

"A Room Full of Paper Souls" and "Blue Island" were previously published in *Alien Buddha Skips the Party Vol. 2* anthology from Alien Buddha Press.

"Westley Heine has been around the track with his original voice. He carries the poetry forward, making what is difficult seem easy. Heine writes of the most commonplace occurrences as if they were images of our "barbaric" and illuminating past. This is a poet to be read and appreciated in our ravaged era. Trust his truth. He will take you by the hand with a firm grip, and like Bukowski and Corso, maintain a rough, cool, and smooth poetics."—Neeli Cherkovski, legendary poet and biographer, author of *Whitman's Wild Children, Hank: The Life of Charles Bukowski, Ferlinghetti, a biography,* and many books of poetry including *Don't Make a Move, Elegy for My Beat Generation, ABC's, Elegy for Bob Kaufman, Hang On To The Yangtze River, Leaning Against Time,* and *The Crow and I*

"Westley Heine's *Street Corner Spirits* is a work of stunning authenticity, wisdom and humanity. It has blood pumping in the veins of its each and every line. There is a whole lot of living in these poems and stories, and Heine weaves them all with marvelous skill under an autobiographical narrative arch that takes you on a journey of survival and self discovery. It's a gritty, beautiful life force of a collection, a revelation to me of a serious talent on the literary scene. I highly recommend this book, Heine reminds me of Raymond Carver, Lawrence Ferlinghetti and Paul Butterfield all rolled into one."—Kevin Ridgeway, author of *Invasion of the Shadow People*

"*Street Corner Spirits* is a great collection of poetry and prose that takes us on a journey from youth memories and shenanigans to the universal mysteries and antics of adulthood. Everything from freaks, love, street people, the dark, the mundane, the apocalypse and Hollywood make their way into the book as Westley Heine and his writing make their way into the hearts of his readers. This is poetry for those looking for their way in this world, and for those that have almost given up ever finding it." —Dan Denton, author of *Finding Jesus & Prayers to my Saints*

"Westley Heine's 'Street Corner Spirits' is a pleasant surprise - an extension of William Carlos Williams' "no ideas but in things" in a similar way to how poets like John Dorsey now toil. The result: we get to go to new and younger worlds and see the data collected. It's a place I've never been and yet recognize, because of its "minute particulars" as William Blake put it -

the details that are vivid enough to take me there."—Marc Olmsted author of *Don't Hesitate: Knowing Allen Ginsberg* from Beatdom Books, and *What Use Am I a Hungry Ghost?*

"Wes Heine is a singer, in every sense, of odd and freaky songs, the kind we always need to hear. With the poems and flash fictions in *Street Corner Spirits*, he captures the memories of an analog youth, the unheeded people on the city streets, and the loving heartbeat of living an open and gritty life." — Kathleen Rooney, author of *From Dust to Stardust* and founding member of Poems While You Wait

"*Street Corner Spirits* by Westley Heine from Roadside Press is a gut-felt heart punch that holds you gasping for air against the ceiling. A young man's coming of age tales, told through poems of hard knocks. Mr. Heine always gets back up and faces the music. Like he's playing guitar or piano with a brick coaxing life and love into the Chicago night. Here's some samplings of his book: "Scar tissue like a burn victim, ghost junkies limp and stagger, cunt is stronger than pussy, cunt is a creating and destroying god, I'm a fuck, a cock weapon of love, city sounds like an ocean, running barefoot in the rain with his mother." This is yet another fine book from Westley that I recommend."—Catfish McDaris, Underground Legend

"As soon as I heard Westley read I immediately was drawn in by the zen AND strength of this person, but he was talking about my life. Extremely parallel. So I reached out, we've become close as I watched his talent flourish, his writing wings spread and fly toward whatever is next. I felt the commonality with him. That we have traveled the same roads in pursuit of better, with prescribed fate, and resilience until there is that "zen" storytellers can groove to. There's music, and Westley is no different than you and I, he just puts one foot forward, then the next.

I could never figure out how he did it, and what was the core of our connection. I could talk all day about the power of this book but I'm not. I don't need to. There are answers here for you, secrets, maybe codes to crack. I know this simply from the preamble where it reads "It's always the same old question: Why write about darkness?"

Why indeed? It's the draw I've had to the man, and artist....Darkness is something we all know and understand. His story IS parallel, and likely is to yours too. He tells us about it, what it's like. How to escape and thrive ... lyrically, with rhythm. And the results are the zen you see and feel in the man. He lives it. Just ask him about his wife. After you get off the floor from the gut punches along the way."—Jack Varnell Poet and Creator/Founder/ Host of the SocialyetDistanced Pod Collective

"From the things we do to stave off boredom growing up in small town USA to the craziness of big city blues, Westley Heine captures every nuance of life in this gorgeous book of prose and poetry. I read it in one sitting, traveled with him through childhood pranks to the madness of the pandemic in Hollywood and on to a certain serenity in Chicago. He writes of each moment with a true poet's skill and insight, bringing the reader through a lifetime of well-placed words and visions that remain." —Nadia Bruce-Rawlings, author of *Driving in the Rain* and *Scars*

"With descriptions that crackle with electricity, Westley Heine takes us through a boyhood of optimism and mischief, a drug-and-alcohol-infused adulthood of living on society's fringes, and glimpses of a life that lands on hard-won peace and joy. Along with these deeply personal accounts, Heine also goes for the jugular in his unflinching renderings of our American moment. *Street Corner Spirits* is an imaginative, high-energy, collection of poems that shows us our complex, destructive, and sometimes healing world."—Mike Puican poet, activist, author of *Central Air,* member of the 1996 Chicago Slam Team, and Board President Emeritus of the Guild Literary Complex

"*Street Corner Spirits* explores family, growing up, small towns, big cities, masculinity, sad stories, bar culture, street culture, drinking, and love. Revealing innermost thoughts and motivations, it goes beyond introspection to social critique, documenting the heartbreaks and hypocrisies of our times in language inspired, clever, skirting the boundaries of the surreal and hyperreal."— Elizabeth Harper, Chicago poet, author of *Love Songs from Psychopaths* and *A Mercenary Girdler*

"In *Street Corner Spirits*, Westley Heine takes us to places we probably don't want to go, from *towns too small for our hearts,* to the viscerally anonymous darkness at the core of Chicago, LA, Paris, and every other city where the only difference between lust for life and a death wish is a last drink at a closing bar or an epiphany of rare, clean air. It's not a comfortable journey, but what keeps us stumbling through this profane *Pilgrim's Progress* is Heine's fearless vulnerability and burning humanity, even as the inhuman seeps from every sweating warehouse wall. Importantly – *vitally,* in all senses of the word – these poems and vignettes have the heartbeat, the street beat, the *Beat* beat of a twenty-first century truth that can't be covered by creeping gentrification and putting on a collar and tie for the daily digital grind. And that truth is that we are all – every single one of us – *shadow boxing with the void*, and we're only just ahead on points. Yet, in spite of this – *because of this?* – there is hope here, and even a quiet redemption of a kind; for, although *there ain't no going back home,* there is a way through. It's not an easy path and there are no easy answers, but if there's one constant in Heine's writing, it's his raw honesty, and when, even as we're caught *in the middle of everywhere, the frontline of nowhere,* he points to the *shores of love* stretching out through the clearing smog, it's something we can trust in."—Oz Hardwick, International award-winning poet, Professor of Creative Writing at Leeds Trinity University (UK), and at-best adequate bass guitarist

"I wouldn't ever lie and tell you that Westley Heine is a terrible poet because quite frankly he's a great poet whose capabilities outweigh the farty old famous living and dead poets combined, in capturing that gritty, unabashedly unbridled spiritual soul essence of the human experience itself. And that's what a poet should be doing. Hands down, Westley Heine is a poet's poet. And I love him alone for that."—Sid Yiddish, Poet, M.A. in Interdisciplinary Studies, Throat Singer, Compductionist, Journalist, Multidisciplinary Performer

MORE ROADSIDE PRESS TITLES:

By Plane, Train or Coincidence
Michele McDannold

Prying
Jack Micheline, Charles Bukowski and Catfish McDaris

Wolf Whistles Behind the Dumpster
Dan Provost

Busking Blues: Recollections of a Chicago Street Musician and Squatter
Westley Heine

Unknowable Things
Kerry Trautman

How to Play House
Heather Dorn

Kiss the Heathens
Ryan Quinn Flanagan